Secrets of the Under-Under World

water

Secrets of the Under-Under World

water

by P.S. Whatever

P.S. Whatever
Secrets of the Under-Under World: Water

First edition

ISBN 978-1-7773196-8-7

Book design: Stephanie MacDougall
Illustrations: P.S. Whatever
Publishing support: TSPA The Self Publishing Agency Inc.

For my brilliant advisors, Gwen and Ellie, with love.

Thank you also to Annika (my model), Willem (my reader) and Devon (who started all of this in the first place.)

CHAPTER 1

The People

It's not so bad, Sam tells herself. Being stuck on the roof. Alone. In the
dark. Listening to Aunt C snoring like a rusty chainsaw inside. At least
the factory is shut down for the night, so the chunks of grit in the air
are no bigger than raisins. That's a good thing. And, thank goodness, the
wind is blowing from the east, away from the garbage dump.

Not so bad, really. She's a smart girl, she'll figure out a way to get back
inside, even if the window did slam shut behind her when she crawled out
to get Darby's pills.

Ka-BOOM!

Sam jumps. One of those sudden storms sweeps across the sky – the
kind that comes from nowhere, does a lot of damage, but doesn't exist
according to the weather channel.

Jagged streaks of lightning slash through the blackness, shredding the
night air with fiery claws. Hail pounds down on the roof, ricocheting off
the tiles, smacking other hail pellets and smashing down on her again.
Sam crosses her skinny arms over her face. But her arms can't protect her
from the flood of water that buckets down, gallons of slimy water that
stinks like... she'd rather not think about it.

"Hey!" Sam yells, at no one in particular. "HEY!"

From the moment she opened her eyes this morning to feel Gemini's
angry tail swishing across her face, she knew it was going to be a bad day.
Gemini had marched her down to the kitchen to show her the offending
cat bowl, which was full of peanuts. In the sink was the soggy mess of
cat food, and on the table were paper dolls made from the cat food box.

Sitting under the table was Darby, smeared with jam, playing cards with Aunt C, who was wearing one of the kitchen pots on her head.

"She's having one of her bad days, Sam".

"I figured that much out myself. And what about you? Couldn't you clean up a bit?" Sam waved her hand at the disaster in the kitchen —every cupboard and drawer pulled open and marbles scattered treacherously across the floor.

Darby shrugged and looked back toward Aunt C. "Go fish!"

"Arrghhh. Am I the only person who can do anything around here?"

Sam cleaned up the kitchen as best she could before school. *At least we're not expecting a visit from The People,* she thought as she pulled spaghetti from the ceiling fan. *Can you imagine what they'd think?*

Unfortunately, Sam hadn't noticed the envelope sticking out the front of Aunt C's dress.

It was after supper when Sam realized just how much trouble they were in. She had been doing her homework when Gemini pounced on the table and pushed her pencil to the floor. Sam reached for the pencil but Gemini snatched it first. Running upstairs pencil in mouth, the cat twitched her tail for Sam to follow.

Upstairs, Sam had found Aunt C standing in front of the open window, pitching things outside. "Thank goodness you're here, Sam!" said Aunt C. beaming. "You can help me throw these darts. If we get another one in the middle of the circle, we win that teddy bear!"

This was the worst day Aunt C had ever had. It might be days until she was normal again. But Sam didn't have time to think about that because, at that moment, she saw Aunt C reaching for Darby's pill bottle.

"NOOOOOO...!" Sam shrieked, leaping for the bottle just as it sailed through the air. Sam's arm stretched... her hand reached... the bottle kissed her fingers... pirouetted in the air... and dropped gracefully to a final curtsy at the far end of the roof.

Sam stared at Aunt C in disbelief.

"Well, that's done!" chirped Aunt C. "Congratulations, Sam!"

That's when Sam noticed the crinkled envelope peeking out of Aunt C's bodice. Sam grabbed the letter and read the worst news she could imagine: The People were coming to inspect.

Tomorrow!

She had to get the house in order. She had to make Aunt C appear at least somewhat normal. And she had to somehow retrieve Darby's pills before he developed another fever.

Sighing, Sam had crawled out onto the roof. She was barely outside when the window slammed shut behind her. She pounded on the window but Aunt C had already left the room. Almost immediately, the snoring had begun - so loud that neither Darby nor Gemini could hear Sam's cries for help.

———

So now what? Sam asks herself. She sits, clutching her knees to her sopping wet chest. The People would arrive in the morning, warm from their cozy beds and their big hearty breakfasts. They would carry notepads that they would fill with scratches of red ink. They would cluck in horror when they saw the shambles of their lives — and with every stroke of their pens, they would make Sam, Darby and Aunt C feel smaller and smaller, more and more worthless, like dust to be swept into a dustpan.

They would send Darby and Sam away "for their own good." And Aunt C? What would happen to her? Sam shudders. What makes everything worse is that it wasn't always this way, not when their parents were alive. They had lived normal lives then, with regular meals, friends, sleepovers, laughter — but thinking about that only makes her sadder.

But wait. What's that speck down below under the flickering streetlight? Could it be a man? Is it possible that he might help her off the roof — that today might not be the worst day in recorded history after all?

It *is* a man! He shuffles down Sockeye Street with a folded newspaper over his head, trying to shield himself from the rain. Suddenly he looks up. He sees her! He squints and rubs his eyes, not quite believing that there might be a girl up there, as high as the crooked old chimney.

"You're on the roof!" he shouts.

"Really?" People say such silly things. "How about helping me get down?"

"Wait a minute," says the man. "I know who you are. You're that skinny kid who belongs to that crazy lady. I saw her at the grocery store holding a bunch of daisies... and... and... and HAHAHAHA!" Laughter spurts out of him like a geyser. "And she complained that the turnips weren't fresh! She confused daisies with turnips!" Tears stream down his face as he sinks

5

to his knees, laughing in the rainy street. "Isn't that the funniest thing you ever heard?"

"Frankly, no."

The man continues to shake with laughter, clutching his belly.

Sam rolls her eyes. "Are you going to help me or what?"

"Sure, I'll help you." Slowly, he pulls himself up, shakes off some mud, and tries to wipe the smirk off his face.

Without warning, he starts to walk away.

"What? Hey, come back here!"

He turns around and looks at her. "I'll help you, kid. I'll do the best thing possible – report this situation to the authorities." Nose in air, he marches away. "HAHAHA! Turnips!"

Until this moment, Sam has managed to hold it all together. She has put up with Aunt C's confusion. With being humiliated in public. With having to remember everything, think of everything, be responsible for everything. With Darby's fevers and Gemini's yowling and the constant clang of the factory. She's put up with the dry patches on her arms that itch so much she wants to crawl out of her skin. With ugly clothes and bad food and no vacations and hand-me-down school books and kids who cross the street when they see her coming. But this? *This?*

"HOW CAN ANYONE PUT UP WITH THIS?" Sam screams into the night air, at the top of her lungs.

The sky blackens even more. The wind howls.

"Yeah? Well, I don't like it either."

She should have known she couldn't trust the man. Or anyone else. Who cares about a 12-year-old orphan kid the world has forgotten?

Everyone else seems to do a better job of fitting in. Like at school when they have to watch General Hoodwink's weekly podcast. The kids are all ears as he tells them how lucky they are to live in this great country, how crime is down, and family income up. How the country's citizens are happier, healthier and wealthier than ever before – Hooray General Hoodwink! Sam sneaks a peek at her classmates and wonders if she is the only one who doesn't quite buy all of this. All the kids smile and clap – but then again, if you don't smile and clap you get into a heap of trouble.

General Hoodwink. Bah, thinks Sam. Suddenly, she feels like she has nothing to lose. Why pretend that she's happy when her whole world is falling apart? When they drag her away, at least she'll have had one perfect moment of rebellion.

She tugs at one of the roof tiles. With a groan, it separates from the roof. She holds it up... aims it right at the factory tower... and throws it. Ping! A direct hit! She rips off another tile and chucks it at one of the factory windows. Smash! The sound of tinkling glass is intoxicating. Sam laughs hysterically. She's never done anything destructive in her life. But the factory stands for everything she hates: the lies, the pollution, the greed, the starvation wages paid to workers, the smoke that makes them all sick. She knows she shouldn't do this, that she'll be punished... but she doesn't care.

"It's not fair! It's not fair! It's not fair!" she screams, jumping up and down in fury. Now that she's started, she can't stop. She jumps and screams and jumps and screams until she can almost feel her brain rattling in her head.

The house begins to wobble.

Her head begins to spin.

The ground below tilts in one direction... then the next, with sky, earth, and buildings tumbling together in a sickening blur. Panic rises in her chest. Her fingers stretch out, blindly searching for something solid. She inches forward, so dizzy that she can't focus. *Where is the edge of the roof?*

Her hand smacks into something hard. Bricks? The chimney! She leans into it like an old friend, knees weak with relief...

Then it collapses into a pile of rubble. She flies to the very edge of the roof.

Don't look down! She needs something, anything, to grab onto! She claws at the slippery roof tile... her feet dangling in the air... her fingers slowly sliding downwards...

The gutter pipe teases her, just out of reach. Her only chance is to let go of the roof and lunge for it. *Don't think, don't think!* She heaves herself sideways and grasps the pipe.

She is safe!

Every muscle in her body aches as she pulls herself slowly, slowly, up to stand.

Shaking, she clutches the gutter pipe for dear life. Suddenly, she hears

a mighty groan. The pipe breaks free of the house and she falls.
She lands with a thud.
The air leaves her body with a whoosh.

———

It takes her a moment to realize that she is still alive. She can wiggle her
fingers and toes. It hurts, but she can move her arms and legs. She opens
her eyes and sees that she has been lucky enough to fall on a pile of soggy
leaves.

All is good.

Not so good. The ground beneath her is shifting and bucking like
a crazy carnival ride. So it wasn't just dizziness that made the ground
appear to move! It *is* moving!

Terrified, she scrambles to her feet.

Suddenly, a gash opens in the ground beneath her. It rips through the
earth like a broken zipper, spitting chunks of soil from its teeth, spraying
dirt in every direction! Seeping from the gash is a hideous smell – slime,
earthworms and dank, dark, horrible things.

Sam jumps over to the other side of the crack. The soil crumbles
beneath her feet again as the ditch widens. She scrambles away from the
crevice - but it widens faster than she can run. She panics. Trips. Finds
herself hanging onto the side of the cliff.

There, just beyond her grasp, is a sturdy twig. She inches herself up and
manages to grab it. Holding onto the twig, she heaves her body upward.
So far, so good. She swings one leg out of the ditch. Now, if she can just
get her other leg out. *One. Two. Three!* She pushes upward and swings her
other leg out of the hole.

The twig snaps!

She slips backwards... and falls! And keeps falling through the blackness – too surprised to even scream.

CHAPTER 2

Downside Up

A snake slithers across the earth in the darkness. It approaches Sam's inert body... slides up her arm... across her neck....

Sam's eyelid flickers. Her body is trying to tell her something but the message isn't reaching her brain. Her head hurts. Everything is scrambled. Thoughts and memories tangle. The past spills over the present, pulling her farther and farther from the outside world.

While Sam lies unconscious, she is a baby again. Her dad carries her in a baby sling on his back. Her mother hums softly, smiling. They are all in the forest breathing the cool pine air. Baby Sam isn't old enough to talk but she understands what her parents are saying. "We'll make the world a better place for you, Sam." Dad looks at her chubby baby face over his shoulder. "You're the reason we'll never give up," says Mom, leaning forward and kissing her cheek.

Then it all abruptly disappears: the forest, Mom, Dad, everything.

12-years-old again, Sam wakes up with a sob.

Where is she? Somewhere cold, dank and very, very dark. Only a sliver of light far above pierces the blackness. Is this an old well? A mineshaft? She shivers. *Or is this a deep grave?*

Her entire body aches but she knows she can't lie here forever. She lifts her head... feels something slimy wriggle on her chest... twitches... and comes face-to-face with an angry, dart-tongued snake.

Sam leaps to her feet, frantically clawing at her body. Is it still clinging to her? Nausea rises in her throat. She pats herself from head to toe, heart thundering in her chest.

She has to get out of this place.

———

Something or someone is watching her. She shivers.

She can't see anyone, but she knows, absolutely knows, that someone is there. Are they going to pounce on her? Will she hear them coming? She tenses her entire body, ready to punch, kick, bite —whatever it takes to defend herself.

Two pinpricks of light appear in the distance. *Eyes.* The brightest, most intense, glowing amber eyes she has ever seen.

Coming closer to her.

She screams.

Something screams back. Tree branches shake. Suddenly all sorts of creatures pop up out of nowhere. Birds and bats fly in all directions, flapping wings and brushing feathers across her face. Monkeys screech, swinging from tree to tree, somersaulting and springing toward her, teeth bared. A snake slithers over her toes then back again.

Sam screams and screams.

Then all at once - poof! – the wild things vanish. The forest is suddenly eerily still. Aside from a feather up her nose and a scratch on her arm, Sam is not injured. Was the attack a warning? Or a test?

Her eyes are beginning to adjust to the dim light. She can make out trees above her. But something is not quite right. *What is it?*

Suddenly, she notices the top of a tree, the pointy end, is pointing down. All of the trees are pointing in the wrong direction, suspended like huge, green, leafy stalactites.

What kind of place is this?

She has to find out.

Sam takes a cautious step forward in the blackness and bumps into a steep wall of dirt. Up close, she can see scratch marks all down the side of the crevice – fingernail marks! So, she's not the first one to fall!

She sees something else scratched in the dirt: "Persephone was here." Wasn't Persephone the princess of the underworld? And isn't the underworld an evil place? A chill runs up her spine as the thought strikes her. *Isn't that where I am — under the bottom of the world?*

Sam slumps against the wall, suddenly sick to her stomach. It certainly smells like the underworld here: the same stench she had whiffed at the surface but with an even stronger smell of sour gas. She forces herself to push on.

———

Sam has hit a dead end. She has spent the past hour exploring – ducking under treetops, scrambling over rock piles, and watching out for animals preparing to pounce. In all that time, she hasn't seen one single escape route that might lead her home.

Ahead of her looms a steep rock wall.

What now? She steps closer. A tiny tunnel slices through the rock. She drops to her haunches and peers through the opening.

She can see dim light from deep inside the tunnel. It must be a path!

A narrow, airless, possibly dangerous path she does not want to take.

But what if this is the way out?

Reluctantly, she wedges her body into the opening. She barely has enough room to twist around. Shimmying on her elbows, she pushes her body through the tunnel.

The stink is unbearable. She tries to block it out by pulling her T-shirt up over her nose – but then she can't breathe. *Keep going.* Her elbows are raw now from scraping over rocks and dirt. *Keep going.*

Suddenly, the airless tunnel opens wide – she breathes a sigh of relief. She stands but immediately sinks as the ground squishes away beneath her feet. Her right arm sinks into a mire of sticky black muck. Flies buzz around her face. She tries to pull out her arm, but the muck is like quicksand, trapping her left arm too.

She squirms, slowly sinking.

She has to keep her chin up. She can't let that muck get into her mouth!

Then she sees it: a rock not too far away. It seems to be on solid ground, clear of the mud. If only she can reach it! She knows it's a risk because any big movement could drag her further down – but it's her only chance.

She twists her body and lunges toward the rock.

Her knee smashes painfully against it. Her hands claw at the rock, trying to find an edge to hold onto. She heaves her body across it and prays that she won't slip...

She feels herself slipping...

No, no, no!

She manages to hook her arm around the edge of the rock, hugging it tight like a big pillow. *There!* She is safe.

As if to reward her, the sky suddenly opens. Blinding light streams in from a huge round hole at the surface.

But how on earth can she reach the surface? Perhaps someone will throw a rope ladder down?

"Hey!" Sam yells. "HEY!"

Silence.

A giant grey hose appears at the surface.

Garbage spews from the hose: pizza boxes, mouldy bread crusts, plastic bottles, rotting hamburgers, a table and chairs, paint cans, and a huge rat gnawing on a bone. Sam presses herself against the rock, trying not to be swept away by the current of filth.

A metal lid clangs into place above her.

Darkness wraps itself around her again.

———

Sam runs her fingers up the slick vertical wall. Now, she really is at the end of the underground. Far above her is a small opening to the sky, but no way to reach it.

On the dirt wall are scratch marks in sets of five: four vertical lines and one horizontal line across. There are many, many sets. *Someone has been counting the days, or weeks, or years.*

She desperately wants to see Aunt C and Darby. They must be lost without her. What if Darby gets sick? What if the rain leaks inside because of the tiles she pulled from the roof? What if The People take Aunt C and Darby away while she's gone?

She shouldn't have gotten so angry. Perhaps it's all her fault.

There's only one way she can think of to get out and that is up. She jams her heel into the side of the crevice and swings the other heel up as far as she can stretch. She finds a toehold. *Okay, good.* Carefully, she pulls her first foot away from the cliff and then stabs it into another spot. Then she swings her other foot up a bit farther... **the** loose dirt crumbles and she slides all the way back down.

Sam slumps, defeated. There is no way to scale this wall. She will be stuck here for the rest of her life. Until the flesh rots from her bones and there is nothing left of her but a ghostly white skeleton.

Wait a minute. Where are the skeletons? She has covered every square inch of this place and has not seen a single skeleton. So there must be a way out!

Now, all the sloths and bats and creepy things in the underworld can't stop her. She's determined to find the way out so that she can go home. With any luck, she'd be there before The People arrive or at least before they take Aunt C and Darby away.

What is that? The sound of rushing water. Could it really be water or just her own feverish desire? She is so thirsty, the water sounds like music. Her nose quivers like a rabbit's. There *is* something fresh and cold and wonderful in this dark and stinky place. Her tongue sticks to the roof of her mouth, desperate for even a drop of clear water.

She gropes her way blindly, directed by the sound and the scent. The roar of the water now thunders in her ears. She realizes that the sound is coming from below her feet.

At the spot where the sound is loudest, a narrow little passageway leads down. Sam jumps in without thinking, anxious to get to the water. Her knees and legs and hips slide through the hole and then she gets stuck.

Great. Just great.

She wiggles. That just gets her more stuck. She can feel her legs dangling in the air. The lip of the rocky hole bites her waist. This is crazy! At least no one can see her, stuck like a big fat plug in a hole.

When you're in a tight spot, breathe. Where did that come from? She's heard it somewhere before. Then she remembers that it's what her mother used to say — back when she had a mother. Sam isn't sure how valuable this advice might be — after all, her mother managed to get herself killed. But it's worth a try. She takes in a deep breath and then lets it all out very, very slowly.

As soon as she squeezes out her breath, her body relaxes and gets softer. It melts into the rock and then slips free like a wet bar of soap.

No time to think. There's nothing beneath her feet. Sam streaks through the sky in a crazy free-fall, toward a huge, pounding waterfall. Swept into its spray, Sam tumbles downward, bouncing in the wet froth, with teeth chattering from the spray and wind.

The waterfall finally crashes into an icy blue lake, and the force of the impact pulls Sam to the very bottom.

CHAPTER 3

Water and Land

When you're thirty feet underwater and your lungs are about to burst, you see things differently. Did Sam think about how incredibly bad her day had been – the mess in the kitchen, getting stuck on the roof, falling into a hole in the back yard, finding everything downside-up, being swept under a waterfall, and then finally plunging to the middle of a lake? No! She did not think about any of these things because she was too busy trying to figure out how to keep from drowning.

And she didn't want to die.

What she thinks about is how to hold her breath long enough to make it to the surface. How to lift herself up out of the thick heavy water without bursting her lungs. How to stay calm and not panic. Slowly, she pulls herself up, up, up – and finally bursts through to the fresh air.

She gulps big, delicious breaths of it into her lungs. She turns her face up toward the sun and feels the rays kiss her cheeks as her pounding heart begins to slow down.

That's when she remembers that she can't swim.

That's another problem with being an orphan. None of the awful families she had lived with had cared about anything as unimportant as swimming. If they gave her food, they acted like they were doing her a huge favor. And now that she and her little brother were living with Aunt C, well... you couldn't expect too much of Aunt C, because lately, she couldn't remember the difference between the refrigerator and the closet.

It feels like she's sinking. She madly kicks her feet. This churns up a lot of water, but she's still sinking. *This can't be happening.* The water is so beautifully blue. The sky is even bluer. In the distance, she can see the perfect arc of white sand lining the beach and a row of palm trees. This is paradise. She can't die now.

She realizes that her heavy shoes are weighing her down. She struggles to pull the laces open. She manages to untie one shoe before she has to come back up for air. As she breaks through to the surface, everything suddenly changes. Instead of flopping around in the water, she is streaking like lightning toward the shore, left foot first.

Now, she finds herself back under water again. She can see a giant fish with her shoelace in its mouth. The fish has to be six feet long and she is practically riding on it, bulleting through the water.

The ride stops abruptly.

The fish darts away, spitting out her shoelace. She bubbles her way back up to the surface and sees that she is only about twenty feet from shore. Gasping for breath, she swallows more water than air.

In that instant, the moment when she discovers the miracle of this water, she forgets all about her fear of drowning. The water makes her entire body tingle, all the way to her toes. It makes her feel light as air. It tastes sweet like an early morning breeze. She feels strong and hopeful and happy (all the things that an orphan longs to feel.)

Her swimming style isn't elegant, but it works. One arm up, then the other. All the time, she gazes toward shore. She thinks she sees a boy standing on the shore watching but when she looks again, he is gone. Her mind must be playing tricks on her.

When the water is shallow enough — up to her knees — she heaves herself up on shore.

She made it!

And what a place this is! It looks like a poster at a travel agency, but better. Palm trees chock-full of coconuts. Daisies and sunflowers taller than her. Millions of butterflies in unbelievable shades of purple, blue and orange. She wants to explore but she can't move another inch.

She flops onto the wet sand and passes out.

———

Someone is staring at the back of her neck. She can tell, even though her eyes are still closed. Until this minute, she thought she was sleeping in her own bed with her own pillow and Gemini tucked behind her knees.

She cracks open an eye and sees a pair of brown sandals right at eye level. Definitely not her own room!

She lifts up her head and screams.

Not because the boy staring at her is scary. He's not in the least. In fact, he has a serious face that Sam quite likes, with straight brown hair falling down to his brown eyes. Sam screams because she realizes that she is not in fact waking up to a bad dream. She really is in a whole new world. This will take some getting used to.

She scrambles to her feet. This meeting hasn't gotten off to a very good start. She realizes she's not looking her best – sopping wet, stringy hair, one shoelace dangling loose. The term "drowned rat" comes to mind. "I'm Sam," she says, wringing the water out of her shirt and pretending that she looks like a normal human being.

The boy says nothing. Instead, he waves his fingers in the air as if he is playing an invisible piano.

That is most odd. "I'm Sam!" she shouts.

More tapping fingers. Sam stares at the boy. He stares back, waving his fingers all the while. Finally, he inches closer and places his fingers on the side of her neck. She feels the gentle drumbeat of his fingertips but has no idea why this boy would do something so strange.

He steps away and looks at her with expectation in his eyes. Has she failed some kind of test?

She tries again. "Are people friendly here?" she asked. His silence is making her just a little bit nervous.

Again, he taps out some kind of message on her neck. The tapping feels like a soft breeze against her skin—kind of pleasant but definitely *weird.*

A twig snaps behind them. Instantly, the boy turns his head. "So he can hear," Sam realizes. *But why doesn't he speak?*

Apparently, he can hear much better than she can. He seems not the least bit surprised to see the tall girl who suddenly bursts through the palm trees.

The girl squints her eyes at Sam. This is the kind of girl who could eat Sam for breakfast. She is about 13, but clearly trying to look older. She has long legs, sharp elbows, and a sleek sense of style. She reminds Sam of the girls back home who ride in their boyfriends' cars, throwing garbage at her out the window as they roar past.

Checking out this girl, Sam is not about to make the same mistake twice. She knows that people don't speak in words down here, so she uses gestures to communicate. Sam points to herself, then points toward the sky. She smiles, hoping that they will understand that she is from the world above.

The girl scowls and rolls her eyes. "Fantastic," she says in a bored voice. "We finally get someone to visit from up above and it turns out to be another moron like this one." She flicks her head dismissively in the boy's direction.

What? Who is she calling a moron? Sam feels her cheeks reddening.

The girl walks in a circle around Sam as if inspecting an object she might purchase. "Not much for fashion," she concludes. "And obviously, not much in the brains department if she can't even talk."

"But... but I can talk!" Sam sputters.

The girl stops and drills her eyes into Sam's. "Then why didn't you in the first place?"

"Because he..."

"You mean Boyo? *Please.* You're not very smart if you're copying him, are you?"

Sam notices Boyo waving his fingers again. He is trying to tell her something, but what? The other girl notices, too. In response, she wiggles her own fingers by her ears and sticks out her tongue.

"But what am I thinking?" The girl straightens, suddenly looking very official. "You can't just drop into another country without permission. Did someone invite you here?"

"No."

"Well then, you'll need to go see The Great Hildinski. She'll decide what is to become of you."

"The Great Hil-*what*-?"

The girl rolls her eyes, as if Sam had the brains of a cabbage. "Hil— as in a hill you go up. Din — like dinner. Ski — the thing you do on snow. Hil-din-ski."

"And this Great Hildinski is your leader?"

"I suppose you could say that," she says. "But look at you. You can hardly see her looking like *that.*"

Sam looks down at her soaking, muddy clothes. She notices a puddle beneath her feet. Shifting uncomfortably, she wonders if she smells like garbage muck.

"Come. I'll lend you some of my clothes."

With a great sense of purpose, the girl strides off. Sam hesitates for a moment, then rushes after her. As she hurries to catch up, she doesn't think to say goodbye to Boyo or turn to see that he has a frown on his face.

CHAPTER 4

In the Palace

The girl's name is Tonya. She lives by herself in an apartment attached to the house of the Great Hildinski.

"You can think of me as royalty," she announces to Sam, pulling her into the room. "I am the granddaughter of the Great Hildinski — the real one, that is."

It's more like a shrine than an apartment. Dominating the room is a life-size painting of a man in a crimson cape and long silver moustache. "Your grandfather?" Sam asks.

Tonya nods, gazing dreamily at the painting.

"So when do I see him?"

Tonya flops onto the bed. "You don't. You will see the other Great Hildinski. The fake."

This is confusing.

"She — the one you are going to see — married my grandfather. He was the world's finest magician and she stole some of his tricks."

"So why don't I go see him instead?"

"Because he's dead." Tonya punches her pillow. "He died and left me with her. That's why I'm stuck in this place."

Sam visualizes the white-sand beach, the palm trees, and the tall daisies. Not such a bad place to be stuck in. Is there something she doesn't know? "So what kind of place is this?"

Tonya thinks for a minute. "Under-Under? Clean. Pure. Completely safe. That's why I get to live by myself."

Sam doesn't get it. Compared to the places she's lived, this sounds pretty fantastic.

Tonya sighs. "It's just so boring. Everything is love, peace, and flower power. Makes me want to throw up." She opens a drawer and pulls out some clothes. "Here," she says, tossing them to Sam.

Sam slides behind the bed and looks at the clothes. Leopard-print pants? They may look great on Tonya but on her? She'll look like something that should be used for target practice. "Don't you have anything else?"

"Don't be so high maintenance." Tonya starts to file her nails. "Let's not talk about stupid Under-Under fashion anyway. Tell me what's happening above. Paris. London. Rome."

Humiliated, Sam comes out wearing the dreaded pants and a shiny T-shirt that is several sizes too big. Yup, she really feels like talking about fashion in this get-up. Anyway, what does she know about fashion? It's not like she's ever had anything decent to wear. But fortunately, Tonya doesn't need to know that.

———

Back on Sockeye Street, The People peek through the window of the house, trying to see inside. "Guess they're really not home," says the one with the clipboard.

On the door is a sign: "Still away."

For three days in a row, they have stood outside Aunt C's house, trying to get inside to inspect. They have a sneaking suspicion that Aunt C is not a suitable guardian for the children and they are anxious to know for sure. But no one answers when they pound on the door.

It's not as if they have a better place to send Sam and Darby. In fact, they will probably throw them back in with the stray dogs if Aunt C fails to pass the test. The People don't question if this makes any sense – the rule says that kids can't live with crazy old ladies, and The People always follow the rules.

Reluctantly, they turn and go away, but make a note on the clipboard to come back even earlier tomorrow.

Once she is certain they are gone, Aunt C peeks out from the upper window. She is feeling much better now except that she is worried sick about Sam and Darby. Where are they? Not even Gemini is in the house

26

— which is strange indeed, because the cat doesn't usually venture very far away from her food bowl.

And the food bowl has sat untouched now for three days.

The morning after Sam and Darby disappeared, Aunt C had woken up, completely alert. It was the radio that had cut through her fogginess. The minute she heard General Hoodwink's voice on the broadcast, she got so angry that the cobwebs instantly vanished. "So General Hoodwink has finally done something good for me," she thought as she cleaned the house from stem to stern.

But then she had noticed that the children were missing. *And then* she had seen the letter from the People, announcing their inspection that day. She couldn't let them discover that Sam and Darby were missing — so she put a sign on the door that said "Away" and hid under the bed.

The next day, she changed the sign to read, "Still Away." However, she doesn't know how long she'll get away with this. Sooner or later, they're bound to break down the door.

———

Fake or real, the Great Hildinski must like her privacy. Sam gazes at the palace in the distance. Like all the other buildings down here, it is made out of rock blending into the landscape. But unlike the other buildings in Under-Under, it's impossible to miss because it's completely surrounded by a circle of fire.

"Are you sure we need to visit her?" Sam asks. "She hasn't exactly put out the welcome mat."

"Sissy!" Tonya taunts.

Reluctantly, Sam picks up her feet and marches on. Closer, she smells the flames from the torches. Even from this distance she can feel the heat on her skin. How on earth would they get into the palace? The torches are too close together to pass in between them without getting burned to a crisp.

Sam drags her feet, hoping that some kind of miracle will take place before they reach the flames. She starts to actually walk backward but Tonya yanks her by the arm.

No more putting it off. They stand right before the circle of fire.

Beads of sweat form on Sam's face – partly from the extreme heat, partly from terror.

"You go first," says Tonya.

Sam stares into the flames. She knows she is being tested. There must be a way to get through. Perhaps if she gets closer, she'll see a gap in the fire? Carefully, she inches her toe forward. The rubber on her running shoe instantly sizzles and melts. "Yeow! Sam yelps, jumping back.

Tonya bursts into laughter. "I can't believe you did that," she howls, clutching her stomach. "Can't you see that there's no way through the flames?"

"But you said ...?"

Tears of laughter stream down Tonya's cheeks. "Do you believe everything you're told?"

"Of course not," Sam snaps. Of all the kids around, she is the least likely to trust anyone. She's learned the hard way that people are usually looking out for Number One. But how is she supposed to know the rules in this strange place?

Tonya finally stops laughing. "I'll show you. This is how average people get in," she says, pointing out a button on a tree that Sam hadn't noticed before. "When they press the button, they might be let in – or they might not."

Tonya pulls a can out from under her jacket. "And this," she says, ripping back the pull-tab on top of the can and grabbing Sam's arm. "This is how royalty gets in."

Tonya shoots mist from the can that is so fine it sparkles into a rainbow around them. It smells like the forest and sea combined. But there's no time to admire the colors or the lovely smell. Tonya pulls Sam straight toward the fire.

Sam tries to put on the brakes, but Tonya is stronger. Sam wants to scream but it's like one of those dreams where you can't make a sound. Now, she realizes they are actually entering the flames – it is so bright she can barely see. *This is it. This is the end! Goodbye...*

Suddenly, they are out the other side!

Sam checks - not a hair on her head is singed. Not a speck of soot has dirtied her clothes. She isn't harmed at all. In fact, she feels delightfully fresh and cool.

"Isn't it fun being with royalty?" Tonya is already standing by the palace door, smirking. "This is where I get off."

Sam gazes at the palace with all of its towers and turrets. Even without the fire, it looks scary enough. "What do you mean? You're coming with me!"

Tonya doesn't answer. She just squeezes herself into a cranny in the rock and disappears.

———

Creeping down the dark torch-lit passageway, it occurs to Sam that it might have been wiser to ring the button like an average visitor. She is certainly not royalty. And she is certainly not expected. What if someone thinks she is a thief?

Perhaps this is Tonya's idea of a joke – just like when she told her to go into the fire. Tanya is probably having a really good laugh right now.

Not my idea of funny.

Sam scrunches up her hands into fists. This is exactly why she never trusts anyone. Well, there's no way that Tonya is going to win. She will find her way out of this place herself, no matter what it takes. Then, when she's old enough, she'll build her own fire palace back at home. And no one would ever, ever be allowed to enter – particularly not Tonya.

Everything around her is made of stone... the floors, the walls, the ceiling. The stone is so thick and cold that it blocks all of the afternoon light. If not for the torches, she wouldn't be able to see a thing.

She gropes her way against the wall... and then sees light seeping out from under a heavy door.

Sam creeps closer, holding her breath. Heavy bolts and locks secure the door. Something very important must be going on inside, she realizes. She presses her ear against the cold iron door and listens: muffled voices, what sounds like clinking glass, and a whirring noise.

She thinks she hears something else as well, but she doesn't really pay attention. She is too fixated on whatever is happening behind the door.

There is only a split second between the time she hears the first faint growl and the time she finds herself surrounded by a pack of snarling dogs.

Sam pastes her body against the door, afraid to breathe. She heard somewhere that you should never look an angry dog in the eye but there are so many of them, she doesn't know where else to look. All around her, there are bared teeth and gleaming red eyes. She chokes on the foul smell of hot animal-breath. She feels the searing heat from their bodies on her skin. *This couldn't possibly be any worse.*

And then suddenly it is. Far worse.

She realizes that these are not dogs. They are wolves!

CHAPTER 5

The Theft

The largest wolf crouches, muscles twitching. The other wolves immediately drop to their haunches, teeth bared, waiting. Seven pairs of red eyes bore into Sam's skull.

She doesn't dare to move.

Or even breathe.

She tries to keep her gaze lowered but the wolf's eyes are hypnotic. Her eyes drift up to meet his...

He pounces! His weight hits her like a cannon ball, knocking her to the stone floor. Yellow teeth loom over her face. Then everything becomes a blur of grey bristly fur.

Pain. Searing pain blossoms on the side of her face as the wolf's teeth clamp onto her jaw and hold. If she moves even slightly, she knows that the teeth will slice into her flesh. A sob dies in her throat. Other wolves circle around, waiting for their share of the kill. Foul-smelling saliva drips onto her face from their mouths.

Please no.

A high-pitched whistle pierces the air.

The wolf drops Sam like a rag-doll.

Sam trembles with relief. Huddling on the floor, knees to chest, she tries to be invisible.

TAP TAP TAP. The sound is like a judge's gavel, a sound Sam knows she should obey. She slowly lifts her head and stares.

Standing behind the wolves is the most magnificent being Sam has ever seen: a woman who has to be a hundred years old. Her straight hair falls all the way to her knees. It's so white that it blazes in the light of the torches and seems even whiter because of the blue-black raven that sits on her shoulder. With hair so white, she might be an angel – except for the anger smoldering in her eyes.

Now, Sam is afraid.

The wolves part as the old woman comes closer. It is only then that Sam notices one wooden leg visible under the woman's loose suede clothing.

She crooks her finger toward Sam and then turns toward a red door.

Shaking, Sam follows. She watches as the old woman waves her fingers in front of the lock. She can hear clicking sounds as the parts tumble into place and the lock springs open. Sam hesitates in the doorway – but one glance back at the snarling wolves convinces her to step inside.

She gasps. This room is like nothing she has ever seen. Live trees are growing everywhere, heavy with luscious figs and oranges. Silver candelabras with hundreds of burning candles stand in front of a massive stone fireplace. In the middle of the room is a waterfall, cascading into a clover-shaped fountain. And the best part: gigantic silver platters heaping with cheese, bread, fruit, and at least a dozen types of delicious-looking cake.

Sam's mouth waters. She hasn't eaten anything since yesterday. (Not even a scrap of dry cereal or a peanut from Gemini's bowl.)

The old woman motions for her to sit down. Sam tears her eyes from the food and takes a seat in a plush velvet chair.

"Where have you taken it?" the old woman asks in a voice that is quiet but could cut through steel.

"What?"

The old woman thumps on the floor with her wooden leg. Somehow, this is as scary as the wolves.

"I'm from up above," Sam says. "I just want to go home."

"Yes, I'm sure you do. With an even bigger piece of our sun."

"I don't know what you're talking about."

"You don't know about the theft?"

"No."

"Or the missing slice of sun?"

"No."

"So you're not a thief? But you were caught breaking into the palace. Have I got that right?"

"I didn't break in," Sam protests.

The old woman turns to the raven on her shoulder. She whispers something. The bird squawks a reply. Then in unison, they turn their black eyes to stare at Sam.

Sam sweats uncomfortably under their piercing gaze.

Suddenly, the old woman stomps the ground again with her wooden leg. The whole earth shakes. Leaves rattle in the trees. Oranges fall to the ground and split open. "I demand to know your name," she says in a voice of authority.

"Sam." She takes a deep breath. "And I demand to know yours."

The old woman rises to her feet, spreading her arms out wide. The earth shakes again. "I am the Great Hildinski!" she declares.

"The real one or the fake?"

A hush falls in the room. Even the trees and flowers seem to hold their breath, waiting to see what will result from this insolence.

For a moment, the old woman is silent. Then she leans forward, so close to Sam that she can see herself reflected in the old woman's blue-black eyes.

"Want to find out? If I'm the real one or the fake?"

Sam stares into the old woman's eyes. She tries to break away but finds that she can't. There is mystery and excitement and power and magic in those eyes that Sam can't begin to understand.

"If you're the real Great Hildinski, then surely you can tell me the way home."

"I can," the old woman says, with just a hint of a smile on her lips. She raises her right hand. Instantly, the room is full of grey doves, flying in every direction. She lowers her hand and in a flash the doves land in the trees. "I can tell you, but I won't. Not until you tell me the truth."

She is interrupted by a loud knock on the door. A guard enters — dragging Darby along with him! Behind Darby is Gemini, who struts over to Sam and wraps her white tail around Sam's ankles.

Sam's mouth falls open.

How on earth did Darby and Gemini get here? On the one hand, she is so happy to see someone familiar that she wants to cry. But on the other hand, now things are even more dangerous: she has to find a way for them all to escape.

"So," said the old woman. "Now, we have two thieves. Or should I say three?"

The guard releases Darby's collar and disappears back outside. Darby runs to Sam and buries his head in her lap.

———

After hours of interrogation, Sam finds herself still sweating under the intense gaze of the Great Hildinski. She twitches, wondering where they've taken Darby. Are they hurting him? Is he scared?

"AHEM!"

Sam snaps back to attention and sighs. "I've already told you every-thing. About Tonya and the rainbow mist. And falling down the hole."

"But *why* did you fall down the hole?"

Sam just shakes her head.

The door opens and a guard enters, carrying a huge plate of cake and goodies. The smell is intoxicating. He sets the plate on the table.

The old woman motions with her hand. "Please."

Sam's mouth waters as she eyes the food. But this could be a *trick!* She clenches her hands into fists. "No thank you."

"Silly child." The old woman thumps on the floor and the guard appears again.

Sam's eyes follow longingly as he whisks the platter away.

"So if you're not going to talk, I will," says the old woman. "You need to know about Under-Under." She pauses, looking away for a moment before continuing, "And why you're not welcome here."

Sam learns that the colony was founded in the 1960's, when everyone was talking love, peace, and flower power. But way back then, a few smart scientists could already see that the love of money might out-muscle the love of nature and drastic action might be needed to help the planet survive.

So they took their most exciting inventions — including a solar-pow-ered "sun" that only needs recharging once a year — and went underground.

There they devoted themselves to research — work that continues on to this day.

"Now, a piece of our sun is missing," says the old woman bitterly.

"But isn't there enough sun left? It seems bright enough."

The old woman glares at Sam. The raven flaps its wings, cawing angrily.

"For your information, we need both parts of the sun. Otherwise, our colony will be in darkness when our lead scientist goes above to charge the bigger piece."

"I'm sorry about your loss," says Sam. "Truly I am. But I didn't steal the sun."

The Great Hildinski sighs. "I'd like to believe you. But you see, no stranger has entered our colony since the beginning. Not a single person. Not a single time...." The Great Hildinski looks down at Sam.

"...until you."

Sam slowly exhales. This is going to be tough.

———

What neither Sam nor the old woman knows is that a stranger has in fact entered the colony.

In fact, a number of strangers.

All of them evil.

CHAPTER 6

The Lessons

Am I a prisoner? Sam follows the Great Hildinski through the dark hallway. The raven brings up the rear, swooping down to brush Sam's head with its wing from time to time. A warning, to keep her in line.

Apparently, the interrogation is over — for now anyway. But what comes next?

It's clear that the Great Hildinski doesn't believe her. Well, who believes an orphan anyway? The people with the power always decide what is the truth.

The raven pushes Sam back into the big room where her brother and her cat wait. She sees Darby leaning over the buffet table, stuffing goodies into his mouth. Gemini licks her paws contentedly, curled up next to a bowl containing a perfect fish skeleton. Apparently the two of them are settling in just fine!

Sam sighs. As usual, it will be up to her to think for everybody.

She surveys the room, searching for a way to escape.

There. What's that stone panel by the fireplace? Sam studies it through her eyelashes, trying not to be obvious. *Yes — she's right!* There is a stone that is slightly ajar! Through the crack, she can see just the faintest light.

This must be a secret way out!

Casually, Sam moves next to Darby at the buffet table. Here, she stands just inches from the fireplace. She makes a great pretense of examining the fruit in a giant bowl, then picks up a ripe pomegranate.

She throws it as hard as she can right at the Great Hildinski.

Grabbing Darby's arm, Sam yanks him away from the food table. She claws at the loose rock, opening a hole big enough to squeeze through.

She pushes her body into the opening, pulling Darby along and whistling for Gemini to follow.

"Faster," she yells to Darby as they sprint down the dark tunnel. They see a light ahead and dash toward it, even though they have no idea what's ahead. Anything would be better than staying where they were, accused of being thieves.

Sam wonders what the punishment is for theft in this land. She shivers.

———

Finally, they reach the end of the tunnel. They step out into the warm afternoon light – and into the icy grip of the Great Hildinski.

She catches Sam with one arm and Darby with the other. *How can a hundred-year-old woman be this strong?* No matter how Sam wiggles and kicks, she can't get away.

Only Gemini is at liberty. "Do something," Sam pleads with her eyes. Instantly, Gemini complies but what she does isn't exactly what Sam has in mind. The cat turns traitor, snuggling up against the Great Hildinski's wooden leg and purring.

"Wait till I get you home!" Sam threatens the cat.

Gemini always puts herself first. But Sam has to admit that Gemini seems to know who is bad, who is good, and who is likely to fill her food bowl. If Gemini trusts the Great Hildinski, then perhaps the Great Hildinski isn't so bad?

But Sam has more to think about than Gemini. She is afraid that trying to run away has made her look even guiltier. How to prove her innocence now?

Sam sneaks a peek at the Great Hildinski to see how angry she is. The old woman is staring up at the sky.

Sam follows her gaze. She sees the sun, just like at home – except a piece of it is missing. For some reason, this strikes Sam as the saddest thing she's ever heard. Sadder even than being stuck underground, so far from home.

"You. Come with me."

Sam gazes at the Great Hildinski with dread. She reaches for Darby's hand, but the guard pulls the boy away. "More cake?" asks Darby, skipping with the guard toward the palace.

Sam turns back toward the Great Hildinski, afraid to meet those fierce black eyes.

—

Fresh flannel sheets. Gentle humming. Sam is tucking little Darby into bed, breathing in his sweet little brother smell.

Then her eyes pop open.

There's Darby, sleeping in the bed next to hers. Except that he's not a baby any longer. And this place is definitely not home.

Where am I? Then she remembers. She shivers as she thinks about the conversation she'd had with the Great Hildinski that afternoon.

Sam shakes Darby awake. "What are you doing here? Who told you to come?"

"Wh-what?" Darby asks sleepily, rubbing his eyes.

Sam wants to smack him. She feels the full weight of the situation land on her shoulders. Darby and his blundering, happy-go-lucky approach to life! Because *he* never worries, she has to worry for both of them. Because *he* doesn't think, she has to think harder.

Sam jabs at Darby's shoulder. "Why did you follow me?"

Darby is stunned. "Why not?"

"Because it's dangerous, that's why not," she snaps. "I hope you at least had the good sense to bring your medicine."

Darby's face falls.

"Great. Now, what are we going to do?" Sam demands. "What if you get one of your fevers? What then?"

"I don't know. You'll think of something. You always do."

"That's right. *I'll* have to think of something. Why didn't you stay at home, you little pest?"

Darby's eyes crinkle around the edges, like he's about to cry. "I thought you'd be happy to see me. I thought you wouldn't want to leave me behind."

Sam loves her brother, more than anything in the world. And she knows she's not being kind. But she's so worried — and so very angry about being worried. She doesn't know how to say what she feels, so she rolls over instead and turns her back.

It takes her a long time to fall asleep.

———

Sam had meant to tell Darby about what had happened in the forest. But her brother had been so stuffed with cake that he'd fallen asleep the instant his head hit the pillow.

The Great Hildinski had led Sam to a clearing in the woods. "What are we going to do with you?" she'd asked.

"You don't want me here," Sam answered defiantly. "So please, help us find our way home!"

"And allow you to tell everyone up above how to get to us? No."

Sam clenched her fists. "I'm not a spy!"

"So you say."

Desperately, Sam looks for a way of escape. As if reading her mind, The Great Hildinski raises her arm — flames leap up in the distance.

"The way back is difficult," said the old woman, staring at the flames as if in a trance. "And not a path you can find by map alone."

"Then, how?"

"By mastering three sacred lessons."

"I'm ready."

"Are you?" The Great Hildinski was silent for a long time. "You can only master these lessons if you hold no evil in your heart."

"Try me."

The Great Hildinski sighs. "Do you see where I'm standing?" she asked.

Sam thinks this is a silly question, but she doesn't dare say so. "Of course," she replies.

"Then shut your eyes and count silently to ten. Listen very carefully. When you reach ten, point to where I'm standing."

This should be easy. The dry leaves crackling underfoot would give the old woman away. Sam counts to ten, listening very carefully.

But she doesn't hear a thing. Not a *thing.* That must mean that the Great Hildinski hasn't moved. Sam points in the direction where she'd last seen the old woman standing.

"Wrong," says a voice coming from exactly the opposite direction. "Open your eyes."

How can that be? Sam scratches her head.

The raven caws with laughter.

"Try again. Listen with your whole body this time."

Sam focuses every molecule of her being into listening — but not even a whisper. Uncertainly, she points in a random direction.

"Wrong again."

Sam opens her eyes. She sees that the Great Hildinski has traveled all the way to the far edge of the forest. How on earth had she done this? Even with the disadvantage of a heavy wooden leg, she moves more quietly than a mouse.

"One more time. Really, really pay attention."

Sam can hear her own heart thudding, but nothing else. She opens her eyes. The Great Hildinski is nowhere in sight.

"Hello?" she yelled. "Hel-*lo!*"

"Right here."

Sam spins around. The Great Hildinski stands right behind her. She should have felt the old woman's breath on her neck.

"That is lesson number one," says the Great Hildinski. "You must learn to trust your body."

"But how do I do that?" Sam pleads.

"Trust your body," the Great Hildinski repeats, walking away from the forest without looking back. "The guard will show you out."

Sam is no closer to getting home. She has discovered the first skill that she needs but she has no idea how to master it.

CHAPTER 7

Setting Out

The next morning, Sam finds Darby already in the kitchen, grinding oats in a special little grinder. But when she asks him why he's doing this, he doesn't answer. This is how she discovers that her brother isn't speaking to her.

Maybe I was a bit hard on him last night. But as soon as that thought crosses her mind, she remembers how complicated he has made everything by following her. Then she feels mad all over again.

"What*ever*," she says, deciding to ignore Darby. She opens a cupboard, looking for cereal. She sees nothing but jars of rice and grain. *Where do these people keep their food?*

It had been decided that she and Darby would stay with a couple named Grace and Simon. They are very nice people, even if they are a bit strange. Grace is a food scientist. She wears bright tie-dyed kaftans, bakes delicious beet muffins, and has a smile so big it takes up most of her face. Simon is the lead scientist in the colony. He wanders into a room muttering, then suddenly thinks of something and rushes back out to write it down.

Simon also has a habit of kissing his wife on the back of her neck.

"Ick!" said Sam, the first time she saw this kissing stuff. "Ew!" echoed Darby (back when he was speaking to Sam.)

Sam is about to give up on finding real food when Grace enters the kitchen. "Well done, Darby!" she says, taking the bowl of oats from him. Then she whips up a pot of steaming hot porridge with juicy blueberries on top — the most delicious thing Sam has ever tasted.

Sam's spoon is halfway to her mouth when Boyo appears.

She drops her spoon, mouth hanging open.

"This is our son," says Grace.

Boyo nods at Darby but doesn't even look at Sam. He waves his fingers at his mother.

"No, she's not under house arrest," Grace answers. "Innocent until proven guilty, remember?"

Sam shifts uncomfortably. *What's with Boyo?* He was much friendlier yesterday.

Between Darby not speaking to her and Boyo not looking at her, Sam doesn't feel very popular today.

———

The one person who does want Sam's company is the one person she wants to avoid: Tonya. She springs out from the bushes the minute that Sam steps out of the house. "How was your visit to the palace?" she asks, her eyes wide and innocent.

"How do you think it was?" Sam marches away without looking at the girl.

Tonya hurries to catch up. "Oh, come on. You've got to admit, it was funny."

"Funny, my butt."

"I'd have killed to see the old girl's face when she found you there."

"Then you should have stayed. You would have enjoyed seeing the wolves' faces, too."

Tonya grabs Sam's arm. "Wolves? I didn't know about any wolves. I swear."

"Yeah, right."

"I'm sorry, Sam."

Sam spins around. Tonya looks sorry but who knew if it's real?

"You didn't get hurt," asks Tonya. "Did you?"

"No, but..."

"And it *was* more exciting my way, wasn't it?" Tonya is grinning now. "I knew that you weren't boring like everyone else."

Not boring! What a lovely thing to hear. But still, Sam's antennae are up.

"You have no idea how dull things have been for me," Tonya continues, "until *you* came."

"Well," Sam says grudgingly. "You still shouldn't take such risks with other people's lives."

"I know." Tonya looks contrite. "It won't happen again. And I've figured out a way to pay you back."

"How?"

"I have a plan. I know how to help you get back home."

———

Sam squirms. She's always hated waiting. And she's already been waiting for hours to hear about Tonya's plan. "Only after dark," Tonya had insisted. "It's got to be a secret. We don't want everyone getting their paws on our idea, do we?"

Waiting might have been easier if Darby would talk to her. But he had gone off to spend the day with Boyo, marching silently past her, nose in the air. Being snubbed by her brother made her even more homesick for the way things used to be: just the three of them (four counting Gemini), living happily in their funny little house on Sockeye Street. Would things ever be that simple again?

Sam knows that she is glossing over the bad things — like the factory noise and Aunt C's illness — but she is so lonely that she swears she will never get mad again. If only she can go home.

"Sam? Are you with us?" Grace asks. "You seem a million miles away."

Sam sighs.

"Are you homesick?" Grace asks gently.

Sam bristles. No way is she going to talk about her feelings. "Tell me about the Great Hildinski," she asks abruptly.

"She's been our leader since the colony was founded," answers Grace. "She's teaching us the old ways."

"Old ways? How does she know all that stuff?"

"She comes from a lost civilization of artists, healers and warriors," Grace answers. "She's the only one left who knows the ancient secrets – and what brought the civilization to ruin."

"And she was married to the other Great Hildinski?"

"Yes, that was her late husband's stage name. But she was always the one who really understood magic."

Sam is quiet, taking all this in.

"There are other things you need to know about Under-Under," continues Grace. "Starting with our water. It's the most important thing."

Water? Something that comes out of a tap? Or from plastic bottles? What's so special about that?

Grace notices the doubting look on Sam's face. "Here," she says. "Try some."

Sam drinks from the tin cup. Instantly, tingles shoot down to her toes. This water *is* different. She could drink it all day and not get tired of it. If she had water like *this*, she would never want to drink anything else.

Grace smiles. "The reason it's so special is that we've kept the Under-Under world completely pure." She re-fills Sam's glass. "Our food is the same. No pesticides. No genetic modification. No over-processing. Just natural, delicious food like people used to eat a hundred years ago."

"Now, look out the window," Grace continues, "and tell me what you don't see."

"Pardon?"

"Look closely. What's not there?"

Sam thinks this is a very stupid question. Tell her what is not there? The list could be endless: there are no pineapples, rocket ships, pepper grinders, or unicorns. *So what?* But then it strikes her— there are no cars! Not one single car, as far as she can see.

Sam turns back to face Grace. "How do you get around?"

"We walk," Grace answers. "When you walk, everything goes by at the right speed."

"But it must take a very long time to get anywhere!"

"That's one of life's mysteries." Grace opens the oven and pulls out a tray of scrumptious beet muffins. "Sometimes, the more you slow down, the faster you reach your goals."

Grace tosses a muffin to Sam, who takes a bite and closes her eyes with pleasure.

"Of course, we also have the magnetic train," Grace continues. "It's one of Simon's most important inventions because it doesn't consume any of the earth's non-renewable resources. In just three seconds, it can speed from one end of the colony to the other."

"Now you're talking!" Sam exclaims. "Who wants to walk anyway?"

"Most of the people. Most of the time."

Sam doesn't understand this at all.

———

Sam tiptoes out the door into the darkness, peeking back over her shoulder to make sure she isn't seen. So far, so good...

Gemini suddenly wraps herself around Sam's legs, purring like a freight train.

"Hush, Gemini," she whispers.

Instead of shushing, the cat makes an even louder noise, "Hnf! Hnf! Hnf!" Is the cat laughing at her? It would be just like Gemini. Sam pushes her away angrily, stepping further into the darkness.

SPLAT! Sam falls.

"Hnf! Hnf! Hnf!"

Sam pulls herself to her feet, scowling. Gemini actually tripped her! *Why on earth...?*

Then she understands. Gemini does not want her to go meet Tonya. The cat nods her head toward the house – her message is clear.

Am I crazy? Gemini is just a cat.

And yet...

She remembers the time when Gemini led her to a little wooden box hidden in the corner of the attic. It was wedged behind some old hat boxes, the hinges so rusted Sam had trouble at first getting the creaky hinge to give. When it opened, she knew instantly that it had belonged to her mother, who had grown up in the very same house. How she knew that, she wasn't sure – she just knew.

Inside was nothing terribly special: a bright green rock, a blue one, an old arrow head, a penny dated 1957, and some rock-hard pink bubble gum. Sam stroked each one of these things in turn, letting them press against her palm like they had once pressed against her mother's. It was comforting to know that her mother had collected stuff like this, just like she collected stuff now. But the real treasure was a photograph, taken when she was exactly Sam's age. On the back, in spidery black writing, were the words, "Anne. Age Twelve."

What a nice face, Sam thought. The photograph was faded, but Sam could see brown hair and enormous hazel eyes. Her mother was standing next to the front stairs of the house. She was as tall as the fifth stair, exactly the same height as Sam now. *So she had been short as a kid, too.*

Sam had stared at the photo. *Such a nice face.* But one thing confused her. Why did her mother have exactly the same features as she did — except her mother was beautiful and she was plain?

Sam wishes she had the photo with her now, to comfort her in this strange place. But the box is in her bedroom back home. And she is here, all alone.

Hnf! Hnf! Hnf! As if telling her to quit feeling sorry for herself, Gemini struts past. Again, she nods her head toward the house.

"Mind your own business, Gemini." Sam sees Tonya emerge from the bushes in the distance. She strides toward the other girl, leaving a worried-looking cat behind.

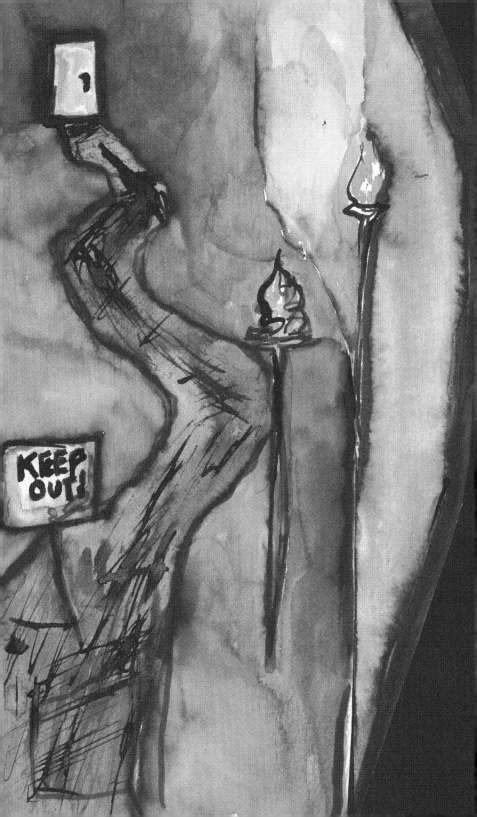

CHAPTER 8

Seven Flags

Sam reaches Tonya and grabs her arm. "Okay," she says. "Spill."

"Not here," Tonya whispers.

Silently, Sam falls into step beside her. They creep across the country-side, under branches, over hills, and far from the houses where people might see them. They keep hiking until it seems that they're in the middle of nowhere.

Sam is getting irritated – this secret squirrel business of Tonya's is going too far. "So, what? Are you afraid that the mice are going to hear us?"

"It's not something I can tell you here. I have to show you."

"What? Is it a map or something? Is it in the forest?"

"Not exactly."

"Then where?" Sam looks through the trees. They can just see the first turret on the palace. "Oh, no," she says. "Not the palace again. No way."

"Do you want to find your way home or not?"

"Are you completely crazy? Have you forgotten that there are wolves in there?"

"I thought you had some spunk."

"Spunk, yes. Death wish, no."

"Do you have to take the fun out of everything?" Tonya grabs Sam's arm and pulls her toward a clearing just ahead. "All right, then. You'll see why you don't need to be afraid."

They march along in silence – until a frenzy of howling cuts through the air. Sam glares at Tonya. "Is this supposed to make me feel better?"

Tonya doesn't answer. If anything, she picks up her pace, almost galloping toward the sound of the wolves.

When they reach the clearing, Sam suddenly understands. The wolves are in a cage. Just seeing Sam again makes them salivate – but they can't get to her.

"How did you manage that?" she asks, full of admiration for this unpredictable girl.

"Let's just say that I have a friend who helps me." Tonya teases one of the wolves with a stick. "Come on. We don't have a lot of time."

They walk in silence until they reach the gate. In the darkness, the palace looks even more forbidding.

"How do I know that you aren't setting me up again?" Sam looks hard into the other girl's eyes.

Tonya smirks. "You don't."

Sam turns to leave but Tonya holds her back.

"You don't know anything in life for certain. But this is as sure a bet as they come."

"Says you."

"Says the person who's thought it through. Look, I want exactly the same thing you do. To get out. To go above."

"Why do you need me?"

Tonya kicks a stone with her foot. "Okay, you may as well know. I haven't been able to figure it out yet on my own. Two heads are better than one."

This seems reasonable enough. After all, Tonya is stuck in Under-Under, which is not at all where she wants to be. If she knew how to go above, she would have already done it. She probably does need her help.

"Okay. On one condition." Sam holds out her hand. "I handle the rainbow can."

She can see that Tonya doesn't like this at all. She grips the can even tighter for a moment – before reluctantly handing it to Sam.

Sam grins. "So, this is what it feels like to be royalty," she says, pulling back the tab.

———

Without the snarling wolves, things are a good deal less stressful.

The girls tiptoe toward the door with the seven locks and bolts. Tonya presses her ear against the thick wood and listens. She smiles... then waves for Sam to follow her further down the hallway.

"What?" whispers Sam, dying to know what Tonya heard. "What's behind the door with the locks?"

"That's where the scientists work."

"So that's where we're going."

"No. What we're looking for is somewhere else."

They creep forward again until they reach the red door leading to the Great Hildinski's inner sanctuary. "Here," Tonya says. "Now, we just have to figure out the lock."

"You've got to be kidding me. We are not going in there!"

Tonya waves her fingers in front of the lock just like the Great Hildinski had done but nothing happens. Tonya sighs with disappointment but Sam is relieved. "Oh well," she says to Tonya. "As much as I'd like to see inside, I think we'd better...."

Tonya pulls a big bunch of keys out of her pocket. Sam's heart sinks as she realizes that she's not going to get an easy out after all. "It would have been much more fun the other way," Tonya says, finding the right key and slipping it into the lock.

Now, Sam feels like she really is a thief. Here she is, in the old woman's private home without an invitation. She thought that they were just going to the palace — that wouldn't have been so bad. But to sneak into someone's rooms? A guilty sensation churns in her stomach.

Guilt doesn't seem to be a problem for Tonya. The girl surveys the place as if she owns it. She picks up an apple, takes a bite, and discards it for a new one.

"Are you sure she's not here?" Sam asks Tonya anxiously.

"Yup," replies Tonya, poking her nose into the Great Hildinski's desk. "She's in the locked room with the scientists."

"You mean she's right down the hall?" Sam is going to throw up. This can't be happening. What if they are caught? Then how likely would the Great Hildinski be to help her?

"Let's see what the old bat is hiding," Tonya says, plunging open the velvet curtain that covers the entrance to a more private room. Immediately, she begins opening cupboards and rummaging through the contents.

Sam hesitates in the doorway. "I don't think we should."

"Too late now," Tonya says, pulling Sam into the room. "This is where we're going to find it."

No point wasting valuable time fighting about it. Sam casts a worried glance back at the door. "What are you looking for?"

"Anything." Tonya sounds disappointed. "Some old letters, maybe. Some nice juicy gossip. She doesn't seem to keep much."

Sam picks up a photograph of the old woman with Tonya's grandfather. In the photo, they both look very happy.

Tonya notices the picture in Sam's hands. "She didn't deserve him, you know."

Wisely, Sam keeps her mouth shut.

"You should be careful of her." Tonya continues. "She may act like she's on your side, but you can't believe her."

After their conversation about the missing slice of sun, Sam had started to think that the Great Hildinski might be okay. The old woman had started to tell her about the three lessons after all. But was she really trying to help? Or was she using her somehow?

Sam hears voices in the distance. Her palms begin to sweat. "They're coming," she whispers. "Be still."

Both girls freeze like statues. The voices outside get louder. They can hear footsteps, now, and laughing. Sam glances anxiously at the velvet curtain. If anyone so much as peeks inside the room, the open curtain would give them away.

She has to close them. Slipping off her shoes, she slides forward in her stocking feet, stepping on a squeaky floorboard almost straight away.

Tonya shoots her a sour look. Sam shrugs, stuck in the middle of the floor, afraid to move another inch.

The footsteps stop — right outside the door.

"Did you hear something?" asks a voice she recognizes as Simon's.

Sam holds her breath. Her heart is beating so loudly, surely they must hear it? The clock ticks. *One second. Two seconds. Three.* The silence stretches. She can't stand this any longer. She's certain she's going to scream.

"Nah," says another scientist. "You must be imagining things. You're nervous because of that break-in."

"Maybe so. But I still can't believe that Sam is the one who stole our sun. Seems like the kind of girl who you could trust."

A knife of guilt stabs Sam's heart.

"Come on, there's no one here," says the other scientist. "Let's get back to our work."

Sam slowly lets out her breath. Thank goodness, it's not The Great Hildinski outside the door! She wouldn't have been so easily fooled. Not only could she move without making a sound, but she could probably hear an insect walk. Not to mention her other powers — making birds fly, the earth shake, and who knows what else.

"We'd better hurry," says Sam. "I'm not going through that again."

"You act like it was my fault. You're the one who made the noise."

"And you're the one who got us here in the first place."

"And you're the one who I *thought* wanted to go home. Guess I was mistaken." Tonya examines her fingernails, as if she could care less what Sam might say.

Sam notices something about the far wall that looks funny. She stares at the far wall but can't see anything really wrong. Still, something niggles at her. On impulse, she leans upside down and looks back at the wall from between her legs. That's when she sees it! A stone of a different texture than the others. There must be something behind that wall!

She shoves her finger into the corner of the stone and presto! It springs open. Behind the stone is another room. "Aha!" she crows. Her entire body tingles with excitement. She is certain that she is onto something big.

She slips through the opening into the room, leaving Tonya baffled behind her.

Inside the room, Sam gasps. It's almost too good to believe: a huge map of the world, right in the middle of the room, with seven red flags stuck in seven different continents.

Seven flags. There must be not one entrance to Under-Under, but seven!

She is so excited she can barely breathe. Surely, if she has seven chances, she can find her way home!

Except...

What if she were to choose the wrong exit and end up somewhere in Africa? Her excitement fizzles. She realizes that she has to be very, very careful, whatever she does.

She examines the map. There! That must be the exit closest to her home. A shiver runs through her body. Not only is the exit close to home — it's right *under* her house.

The red flag is labeled Sockeye Street ... her street. On the flag is a little picture of a house - her house.

Somehow, all of this has to do with her. Sam shivers again.

CHAPTER 9

The People Tank

Meanwhile, back above the surface of the earth, General Hoodwink is giving another speech. He struts across the stage, thumbs hooked around his belt, necktie resting on his flabby belly, a smile stretching his lips across his teeth. But his smile does not extend to his eyes. His eyes are cold, blue and utterly without humor.

"I have an announcement," he yells, not trusting the microphone to do its job. "A very important announcement!"

The crowd watching the speech in General Hoodwink's castle leans forward. In living rooms around the country, old women stop their knitting and men wake up from their snoring. In cafes and laundromats and office buildings, people crowd around television sets, computers and phones. In the classroom — where Sam is notably absent — kids squirm in their desks, knowing that they had better look happy, really happy, even though they're bored to tears by blah-blah-blah they hear booming through the speakers.

THWACK! Teacher smashes her pointer down on a desk. Now, the kids grin nervously, trying to look interested. No one even dares to blink in case the split-second closing of an eyelid is seen as bad behavior.

"My fellow citizens!" yells General Hoodwink. "There are those among us who believe that our fair country is not doing enough to save the environment! But this is a lie!"

Silence prevails throughout the country as everyone waits to hear more.

"I am pleased to announce the most brilliant program, the most progressive plan that any country has ever devised. We are the new leader in 'green.' We are the new leader in 'clean.' Announcing my "Under the Rug Plan!"

"Ever heard of that?" a reporter whispers to a colleague, who shakes her head.

The State Scientist hobbles onto the stage, wheezing into his handkerchief. "Here is our plan," he says, blinking at the crowd over his glasses. "We take all of our carbon, all of our pollution, all of the bald tires that clutter our countryside, all of our waste – and we pump it all underground!"

"We have successfully completed our first test dump," adds General Hoodwink, "We sealed seven tons of garbage underground! Hurray!"

He claps his hands fiercely. His Ministers pick up the clapping and then everyone joins in, everyone in the whole country, clapping so hard their hands hurt.

Almost everyone, that is. In the classroom, two of the kids (Sam's only friends) don't feel like clapping. They look at each other and shake their heads.

———

Down in Under-Under, there's a significant lack of clapping.

Tonya has finally found the secret entrance to the room. She scowls when she find Sam still staring at the map. "Great," she says, pursing her lips. "How does this help us?"

It's a good question. They had discovered the map but all it told them was that there were seven points of entry to Under-Under. It didn't tell them a thing about how to get back and forth between worlds. No matter how hard Sam and Tonya search, they can't find anything that sheds light on the situation.

Perhaps the answer is on the map itself? Sam looks carefully at each of the flags: one in North America, right in her home town of Lost River; one in South America; one in Africa; one in Asia; one in Europe; one in Oceania; and one in Antarctica. Reverently, Sam whispers each of the continent names.

"Grow up," snarls Tonya. "Who cares about these places? We're no farther along than we were before."

Sam has to admit that this is true. Still, these names must be important. She is sure that they are part of the puzzle.

———

Sam sneaks back into Simon and Grace's house, quietly closing the door behind her. Inside, she leans against the door, listening.

She can hear the frogs' ribbit outside... the breeze in the trees... even Darby's gentle breathing. She steps forward softly, ears alert but hears nothing else. Nothing! She takes another step, expecting to see Grace on the step with a candle – but no. She has managed to move so quietly that no one has heard her enter!

Does that mean that she has mastered the first lesson? Proudly, she takes another step forward – and the floor squeaks.

———

In the morning, Sam is grinding oatmeal when Boyo enters the kitchen. He stares at her, his mouth pulled down at the edges. "What?" she asks irritably, turning her back.

"I saw you and Tonya last night."

Sam keeps grinding, staring at the oat flakes. It takes her a few minutes to realize that she has heard Boyo speak. She spins around and stares at the boy.

"I saw you," he repeats.

Watching him, she realizes that he is speaking with his fingers, same as always. But she can hear him!

"You can talk!"

"Of course. I've always talked. It's you who's learned to listen."

"Tonya doesn't understand you, does she?"

A dark look crosses Boyo's face. "I don't want to talk about Tonya. And don't change the subject. I saw what you two were up to last night."

"We weren't up to anything." Sam lowers her eyes. Not a very good liar.

"I can prove it."

"Sure, you can." With more bravado than she feels, Sam struts from the room, leaving the oatmeal job half-finished. In the doorway, she almost bumps into Darby, who has clearly been eavesdropping.

"You were talking to yourself," he says.

66

"No, I wasn't. I was talking to Boyo."

"But Boyo doesn't talk."

"You can't understand him?"

Darby looks at Sam like she's crazy. Then suddenly his face changes. "Don't think I'm not still mad at you."

"Aw, Darby. I'm sorry I yelled at you."

Darby pouts for a moment, and then softens. "And I'm sorry I forgot my medicine."

"It's okay. I'll think of something."

Darby grins. "You always do."

———

That whole day, Sam stays out of Boyo's way. Maybe if she avoids him long enough, he'll forget all about what he saw last night.

No such luck.

"Come on," he says, pulling her down from the ladder where she is picking apples. "I have something to show you."

His hand is warm and comforting but she shakes it off. Walking silently alongside him, she is more curious than anything. But then she sees where they are headed and abruptly stops.

"Not the palace."

"I *saw* you. So you owe me this."

Just before they reach the palace, Boyo takes a sharp right. Instead of going through the fire, he scrambles down a steep bank. Sam stumbles along behind him, loose pebbles spraying out from under her shoes.

At the bottom of the bank is a huge cave.

Sam stares into the blackness. She can feel the coldness of the air from where she's standing and she shivers, only partly from the cold.

But then something occurs to her. "Is this another way into the palace?" *Maybe this is where she will find the hidden legend to the map?*

"Not into the palace. But close to it."

A little ways into the cave, Boyo stops. "There," he says, pointing upwards.

Blinking in the darkness, Sam finally sees a narrow opening in the rocks. She creeps closer. Now, she can see the palace and the ring of fire through the gap. A secret lookout! Anyone approaching the castle would be visible from this spot but anyone hiding down here would be completely hidden.

"Where did Tonya get the rainbow mist cans?" Boyo suddenly asks.

"I don't know. She says that she's royalty."

"Royalty my foot." Boyo scowls. "Let's keep going."

So there was more to his plan than just proving that he had seen her enter the palace. Sam follows him through the cave, descending deeper and deeper as the cave gets darker, colder, and clammier.

Finally, they reach a rough-hewn doorway. "Ready?" Boyo asks with a slight smile on his face.

"Huh?"

Boyo takes her grunt as a 'yes.' He puts his shoulder to the door and heaves as hard as he can. Slowly, stone grinding on stone, the door inches open.

Sam gasps and blinks. The light is incredibly bright after the dim cave. She sees that they are in some kind of aquarium. There are glass walls on all sides of the room, through which Sam can see turquoise water, orange coral, and ivory-white clams at least eighteen inches across. She has never seen anything so beautiful. Tears prick her eyes.

"Where are we?" she asks.

Boyo holds a finger to his lips. She falls silent.

Then he begins waving his fingers, but so softly that all Sam can hear is a whisper. As he flutters his fingertips, fish of every size, shape and colour swim toward the glass: tiny electric-blue ones, flat ones with both eyes on top of their heads, ones with lacy fins in wild colours like lime green and yellow, and striped and polka-dotted ones.

Sam turns to face Boyo, a question on her face.

"It's a people tank."

"You mean that all the fish come to stare at us? Just like we usually stare at them?"

"Exactly. They're the ones who are free. We're inside the glass."

Sam notices a huge fish.

"That's the kind of fish that pulled me ashore!" she exclaims. Immediately, all of the fish flip backwards from the glass, as if they've been attacked. Boyo frowns at her—she has been too loud.

"Sorry," she mouths.

The fish glide back toward the glass. She watches, fascinated. They dance a sort of water ballet, fins brushing against tails, slim bodies gliding through the clear water, round fish lips making kissing gestures. Every time Boyo raises so much as a finger, more fish join the dance.

"You speak their language," Sam whispers.

"In the old days, that was normal."

Then Sam notices a row of grey stone rocks shaped like tombstones. "What are those?" she asks.

"Tombstones."

Sam gives Boyo a puzzled look.

"They're for all the species of fish that were lost."

"Lost?"

"Gone forever," Boyo says sadly. "Look, here come the salmon. These ones make me the saddest."

"Because people eat them?"

"No. Being part of the food chain is being part of nature. I feel sorry for them because they don't know how to die."

This makes no sense to Sam.

"Every salmon is born in a particular stream. When they're big enough, they go out into the ocean and live their lives. The strong and smart ones survive — then come back to their stream to spawn, create another generation, and die."

"What's so sad about that?"

"When these old ones tried to go back to their stream, it wasn't there anymore."

"So they can't spawn. Or die in peace?"

"Exactly."

They are both silent for a moment, watching the sad old fish swim around in circles.

"I have a question," she says. "Was there a stream straight above here that doesn't exist anymore?"

"Oh yes. A big one."

Straight above where they are standing is Sam's house.

Suddenly, it all makes sense. No wonder her neighborhood looks so sad. There was supposed to be a big, gushing stream where the grey factories stand today.

No wonder her town is called Lost River.

"Fortunately," Boyo continues, "most of that stream made its way down here. I can show you."

So, her stream is still alive! Sam tingles with excitement. This stream must be part of the puzzle that will take her home!

She simply must see this stream with her own eyes – right now.

CHAPTER 10

At the Far End

Before they leave the cave, Boyo leads Sam to a steep, narrow rocky passageway. She scrambles up behind him, careful not to slip on the wet stones. At the top, she squints in the darkness and sees a huge telescope sticking through the rock, pointing upwards.

"We can see what's happening up above!" Sam exclaims.

"Yes," Boyo answers, "but not on the ground. We can see the surface of the ocean."

Sam gazes through the telescope. *It's so beautiful!* Majestic rolling waves. Sea spray. Sunlight sparkling on the water. Then Boyo nudges the telescope to the right...

"What?" Sam pulls back in horror. Then she looks through the scope again — at a huge lake of plastic bottles and garbage.

Her knees suddenly turn watery. She didn't know she could feel such grief over an ocean! Boyo grabs her hand and squeezes.

"Come on," he says softly. "Let's go see your stream."

Outside, Sam fills her lungs with fresh air. She can smell wild rosemary growing on the hill. And she can hear water!

Excited, she turns to Boyo but he is strangely quiet. Something seems to be troubling him. But what?

Below them is the stream. "It's a nice stream," Sam tries to tell herself, but really, she is disappointed. The stream isn't nearly as big as she had imagined. In fact, when she looks closer, she sees that it starts out okay but then dwindles down to just a trickle.

"I knew something was wrong," says Boyo. "Come on."

They slide down the bank as quickly as they can. When they reach the stream, they look at each other, puzzled. It's as if someone has performed a magic trick — a magic trick of an evil kind. The stream literally disappears before their very eyes.

Sam takes off her shoes and socks. Where the stream begins, the water feels wonderful on her feet — she loves squishing her toes into the mud. The water comes up to her knees... then to her shins... then to her ankles... and then there isn't enough water to wash the mud off her toes.

She walks back toward Boyo, perplexed. But before she reaches him, she crumples over in pain.

"Yeow!" Sam grabs her toe, which throbs so much it makes her cross-eyed. She must have stubbed it on something — something very hard. She bends down to inspect.

There. Right at the edge of the stream, something shiny. "You'd better come here," she calls to Boyo.

Boyo squats on his haunches and examines the edge of the stream. Camouflaged under some weeds at the side of the stream is a big, steel pipe.

"Someone is diverting the water!" Sam exclaims.

"Diverting, nothing. Someone is *stealing* the water."

They trace the pipe down the hill and across the meadow. The farther they walk, the madder Boyo gets. "Why those dirty rotten..." he shouts with his fingers, until Sam has to cover her ears to block out his shouting. Angrily, he shoves his hands in his pockets and, once again, all is quiet.

As for Sam, she is more confused than anything else. She believes that the stream has something to do with her going home. But now, it seems that things are even more complicated.

They continue walking. Walking and walking until their feet ache.

"This could go on forever!" Sam says, discouraged.

"Let's stop and think. If you had stolen something, you'd want to take it as far away as possible, right?"

"Right."

"Particularly if the whole colony depends on the thing that you'd stolen."

"Right again."

"And *especially* if the thing you'd stolen is big enough to fill a dozen swimming pools."

"*Right.* So what does that mean? Where is it?"

"I don't have a clue," admits Boyo, shrugging.

"The magnetic train! That's got to be it."

"How do we know where to get off?"

"How about the end of the track?"

Boyo looks at her like he's going to argue, but then sighs. Sam sees that he doesn't have a better idea.

"It's a shot in the dark," she says. "But it's better than doing nothing!"

Not too far in the distance, they see the nearest train station. They look at each other — then run to catch the train.

———

"Oh, my goodness," exclaims Sam. They are barely in their seats before the train stops. The passenger door flings open.

"We're here?" Sam's eyes wide with surprised disbelief.

"Where else could we be?"

"Don't be smart. That distance would have taken hours to walk!"

"Days, actually." Boyo jumps off the train, pulling Sam behind him. "But sometimes, the slower you take it, the faster you reach your goals."

"I know, I know. Grace told me."

"Sam?" Tonya's sharp voice slices through the air, making both of them jump. "Is that you? You're just the person I want to see!"

They hear footsteps crashing through the bush.

"Although I think you're a bit crazy," Tonya's voice continues from the bushes. "You're talking to yourself, you know."

Sam and Boyo exchange a look.

Out of the trees pushes Tonya, looking like a happy jungle girl. Her smile disappears as soon as she sees Boyo. "What are you doing with the village idiot?" she snarls.

Boyo reddens. Sam shifts uncomfortably.

"Ask her what *she's* doing here," says Boyo.

"What are you doing here?"

"I don't know," answers Tonya. "What are you doing here?"

"Don't tell her," Boyo whispers. "She might know something about the water."

"I wanted to ride the magnetic train," replies Sam, thinking quickly.

"I didn't expect to see you way out here."

Tonya stares hard at Sam, as if trying to decide something. Then she drops her voice to a conspiratorial whisper. "There's something very strange going on here."

"Something about the water?" Sam asks without thinking. Boyo groans. As soon as the words are out of her mouth, she wishes she could claw them back.

"How did you know about the water?" asks Tonya, suspicious. "I thought you just wanted to ride the magnetic train?"

Sam and Tonya circle around each other, both looking for any sign of weakness. The girls are evenly matched — Tonya is taller and older but Sam has the toughness that comes from taking care of herself.

Finally, Tonya breaks the silence. "I've seen something," she confesses. "There are some men hanging around here, and I bet they're up to no good."

Sam tingles with excitement. So her hunch about taking the train was right! Whatever is happening, it is taking place here, at the far end of the colony. "Where are they?" she asks.

Tonya hesitates, but just for a few seconds this time. "I'll show you," she says.

As Sam and Boyo turn to follow Tonya, the older girl suddenly flips around, scowling. "Does he have to come?"

Now, Sam hesitates. If she betrays Boyo, Tonya will think she's cool. But betray Boyo? She can't do that! "Yes," says Sam firmly. "He's here with me."

"Whatever," mutters Tonya, striding into the jungle. "If you want to hang around with a half-wit, that's your call."

"He's not a half-wit..." Sam protests but she stops short when Boyo interrupts her.

"Let her think that I'm stupid," he says. He looks at Tonya and smiles, knowing that she can't understand. "That way, she'll be less careful about what she says."

This makes sense. Now, Sam just has to remember not to reply to Boyo and risk Tonya thinking that she is talking to herself again. It wouldn't do for Tonya to think that she is a half-wit, too.

They trudge through the jungle for about ten minutes without seeing anything interesting. Along the way, Sam finds a perfect walking stick:

a long straight fallen tree branch that fits perfectly into her hand. She knows instinctively that this is something she should hold onto.

"How much farther?" Sam asks.

"Keep your voice down," Tonya snaps. "These men look dangerous."

Sam notices Boyo gliding over twigs and branches without making a sound, just like the Great Hildinski. She practices softening her step. It doesn't work if she starts with her feet – she has to make herself light in the core of her body first, and then spread that lightness out to her limbs. There, that's better. Now, she feels more confident –until CRACK! She trips over a loose twig and it snaps, loud as a gunshot.

Both Tonya and Boyo scowl at her this time. Sam hangs her head. Obviously, this light-footed stuff is going to take a bit of practice.

"We're getting close," Tonya whispers. "Keep your eyes open."

"Do you think they'll hurt us? Sam whispers back.

"I don't know."

They creep forward a little farther. Now, Boyo leads the way, relying on his keen hearing to alert them of any danger.

Suddenly, Tonya grabs Sam's arm. "If we play our cards right, these men can help us."

"But I thought they were bad guys?"

"They are. But if they're doing what I think they're doing, they can help us find our way above ground."

Sam stares at Tonya, puzzled. "How do you figure that?"

"I think they're going up above themselves."

Now, this is a new twist. But Sam doesn't have time to dwell on it. They hear voices up ahead. They all freeze in mid-step, holding their breath, listening.

"Quietly, now," breathes Tonya. All three of them tiptoe a little closer... and just about throw up!

Right there, about fifty feet in front of them, is the biggest, ugliest, nastiest looking man Sam had ever seen.

CHAPTER 11

Lug

The man is about seven feet tall and almost as wide. He has a round potbelly, hunched shoulders, and long, greasy yellow hair. Despite his enormous size, he has tiny, piggy eyes that squint out from his fleshy face.

Sam can't stop staring even though she knows it's not polite. It's like seeing a car wreck at the side of the road – something so ugly, you really don't want to look but you can't help yourself.

The smell of rank sweat clogs her throat – so thick and heavy that she is afraid to breathe.

"Look," says Boyo in a voice that only Sam can hear. "He's carrying a pipe."

"That's just like the pipe I stubbed my toe on!" exclaims Sam, forgetting that she is speaking out loud.

"Pipe?" Tonya narrows her eyes. "So, there is something you aren't telling me!"

"I thought it was a bit odd," admits Sam, "bumping into a pipe at the side of a ditch."

"So what else are you holding back?"

"Nothing."

"Ask her what *she's* holding back," says Boyo.

"And what about you?" Sam asks. "What are you not telling me?"

Suddenly, the giant stops. He puts down the pipe and peers into the bushes. His piggy eyes scan the landscape from one end to the other. All three kids hold their breath and freeze again.

"Don't say anything," warns Boyo. "There are more of them."

Boyo is right. Now, ten men the size of the giant (although perhaps not quite as ugly) enter the clearing. The smell wafting over from them is almost intolerable. Sam presses a leaf against her nose in an attempt to block the evil fumes.

Sam creeps closer, practicing her new skill. She manages to keep the core of her body very light, gliding forward without snapping so much as a twig. She hides behind a rock and watches.

The men are laying pipe. She can see a rough patch of churned up soil in the middle of the clearing. On either side, the ground is clear, smooth, and covered with moss and leaves. If you didn't know better, you would never suspect that the ground had been disturbed.

She watches as the men lay down five feet of pipe, then five more. They quickly connect the long pipe that leads from the stream near the palace to another pipe. She can't tell where the other pipe goes but she is determined to find out.

Tonya silently creeps up next to Sam. "That's Lug," she whispers, pointing at the first man they had seen. "He's the leader."

"How do you know?"

"I overheard them talking."

The men continue to work. Soon, the two ends of the pipe meet. Then one of the men brings over a blowtorch and seals all of the seams, spraying orange sparks in all directions.

"It should hold water now," whispers Tonya.

As soon as the pipe is sealed, the men begin to camouflage it with dirt and leaves. Then they march away, out of the clearing.

Suddenly, Boyo is at her side. "Quickly," he says. "We can't risk losing them."

As quietly as they can, they follow the men through the forest. For a while, they trudge along familiar landscape but then reach a part of the colony that is quite different. Here, instead of lush vegetation, there are sharp, craggy rocks and heavy, dark trees.

In the middle of the trees looms a monstrous grey granite building, cold and forbidding. All three of them watch as the giant men stomp through the great mouth of a front door.

From inside comes a high-pitched whining noise – a noise that suddenly cranks up from whining to thudding and then crashing.

"Something's happening," says Sam urgently. "Let's go."

Boyo grabs her arm. "Not so fast. We need a strategy first."

"A strategy. Right."

"I don't get you," says Tonya, looking at Sam as though she has sprouted an extra head. "One minute, you say one thing, and the very next minute, something different."

Note to self. I must quit talking to Boyo while Tonya is around!

"Be careful with Tonya," says Boyo, as if reading Sam's mind. "And not just about speaking my language. Ask her how she knows so much."

Sam is about to respond when she remembers: no speaking to Boyo! She composes herself and looks at the other girl. "Tonya," she says, "I told you about discovering the pipe. But you haven't told me what brought you here."

"Oh, you know," Tonya twists a strand of hair in her fingers and looks away.

"No, actually I don't."

Tonya shoots Boyo a dirty look. "Well, I suppose there's no harm talking in front of him, considering that he's an idiot and all."

"Don't react," says Boyo. "Let her say what she wants."

"I saw them building the pipe few weeks ago," Tonya confesses.

"And you didn't tell anybody?"

"Of course not." Tonya picks a ladybug off the tree next to her and squishes it between her fingers. "It's my secret."

"But what they're doing could hurt people."

"Hurt, shmurt." Tonya wipes the dead bug on Sam's sweater. "You're such a baby sometimes."

"Tonya!" Sam looks down at the crushed bug remains on her sweater. "Poor bug!"

"Poor bug!" imitates Tonya sarcastically.

"The giants are stealing the colony's water," Sam continues. "People need water to survive."

"I'm sure there's enough for everybody. What can one little factory do?"

Sam stares hard at the building. "So it's a factory!"

"A water bottling plant."

"No wonder the fish have been upset," interrupts Boyo. "I knew something was wrong."

"What are they planning to do with the water?" asks Sam. "That's a lot of water to trade for beet muffins."

Tonya laughs. "Beet muffins. You slay me."

"Well, if not beet muffins, then what? There's no money down here after all."

"Finally, you get it. I swear, Sam, you've been hanging around with Boyo too much. You're becoming a bit thick."

Sam shoves her hands in her pockets, frustrated. What is Tonya talking about? She'd like to tell her exactly what she thinks of her but she knows that it's more important to play it cool and get some information. "Okay, so you're the smart one," she says finally. "Spell it out."

A smug look crosses Tonya's face. "There's no money down here," she says. "But there's plenty of it up above."

"They're taking the water out of Under-Under?"

"Of course."

"How do you know that?"

Tonya looks away. "I overheard their conversation. I know everything."

"Then aren't you in danger? Those men are awfully big. And mean looking." She would hate to meet even one of them in a dark alley.

"I'm not a coward," says Tonya, nose in the air. "I told you. I'm royalty. I know how to take care of myself."

Sam is not convinced.

"And don't forget. These gentlemen are our ticket out of Under-Under."

Gentlemen? That's not the way Sam would describe them. But maybe they could help her find the way home — if they were willing? "How do we get them to take us up?"

"We outsmart them," Tonya says, lifting her chin defiantly.

———

"Boyo should be the one to go investigate."

Sam can see that Tonya doesn't like this at all. "No way," she protests.

"But he's way quieter than either of us. He has the best chance of not getting caught."

"Maybe, Tonya acknowledges grudgingly. "But what about when he comes back? He won't be able to tell us what has happened."

"Oh, I think he will."

While the girls argue about who should be the one to go, Boyo resolves the issue by simply slipping away. When Tonya turns around, he is gone.

"I suppose he has certain talents," Tonya admits. "Kind of like a seeing eye dog."

Don't react. Don't react. Don't react! Sam hates it when Tonya puts Boyo down but she is learning to keep her mouth shut. She bites her fingernails, waiting for Boyo to return.

Meanwhile, Tonya stares into the distance. "What time is it?" she asks.

"About a minute since you asked me last."

All of a sudden, Boyo is back. Even though both of them had been watching closely, neither of them had seen him coming.

"How do you do that?" Sam whispers.

"It just takes practice."

Tonya notices Boyo's waving fingers. "Oh, I get it. You two have worked out a secret sign language. That's very sneaky of you."

"It's not a secret," says Sam. "You just have to be smart enough to figure it out."

Tonya glares at Sam. But Sam doesn't notice because she is busy following Boyo's moving fingers.

"There are two entrances," Boyo explains. "One straight ahead with a big gate. And another smaller one around the back."

"What's he saying?"

Sam repeats what Boyo has said.

"I know that much already," Tonya says. "Ask Mr. Talking Fingers if he found out anything useful."

"There are guards at both entrances," Boyo continues. "But the guard at the back is complaining about wanting some lunch."

"What?" interrupts Tonya. "What's he saying?"

"What he's saying," answers Sam, "is that we should go around the back."

Boyo and Sam look at each other. They don't need either words or tapping fingers to communicate what they are thinking.

They have a plan.

CHAPTER 12

The Discovery

"Now, I've seen everything." Tonya frowns at Sam and Boyo. "We're planning an attack on the factory, and you two choose this moment to pick berries."

It's true. Both Sam and Boyo are busy hunting under bushes and through patches of grass for just the right specimens.

"Here," Sam says, handing a fistful of fragrant green herbs to Boyo. "Are these ones good?"

"Just what I was looking for," replies Boyo, smiling.

Boyo combines all of the ingredients into a nice, granola-like mixture. It smells absolutely delicious — a magical combination of sweet honey and crunchy biscuit. Wrapping it into a banana leaf, Boyo adds the finishing touch: a fat raspberry bursting with juice and sunshine. "Ready?" he asks, waving his fingers at Sam. She nods. Boyo slips off and the two girls follow at a close but not-too-close distance.

Boyo sneaks up ever-so-quietly until he is about five feet away from the guard. Then he freezes.

The sound of frogs ribbiting in the marsh is deafening as the kids wait, holding their breath.

What if the giant sees Boyo before he gets a whiff of the food? He could wrap one of those beefy hands all the way around Boyo's throat.

The guard suddenly stomps into the marsh and quickly returns, holding a wriggling frog. Sam watches in horror as he pops it into his mouth and swallows.

Sam clasps a hand over her mouth as vomit rises in her throat. But Boyo creeps even closer, until he is only inches away from the guard.

Sam shuts her eyes. *Get out of there, Boyo!*

Carefully, he sets the banana leaf package on the ground and floats back to the place where the girls are hiding.

Sam sighs with relief. Even Tonya seems happy that Boyo hasn't been captured. Now, they simply have to wait.

The guard flares his nostrils. Even from a distance, they can see his nose sniffing the air. But he doesn't seem to notice the package just to one side of his right boot.

It's torture waiting to see if their plan will work. Now, the guard closes his eyes. His nose is madly twitching, as if his nostrils aren't big enough to trap enough of the delicious air. He licks his lips, saliva dripping onto his shirt.

Finally, the guard leans forward and spots the package. He looks over his shoulder to see if anyone is looking... then casually nudges the package closer with his foot. Leaning down, he pretends to inspect his boot... then snatches the package. He swallows it in one gulp and belches.

The guard rubs his belly and belches again, pleased with himself. Fortunately, he makes so much noise belching that he doesn't hear the giggles sputtering out from between Sam's fingers.

"Look," whispers Boyo. "He's falling asleep."

The guard stands, teetering on his feet. His eyelids are so heavy they pull his whole head downward. He leans against the building and slides down the wall, all the way to the ground. He hits the ground with a bump, tucks in his chin, and begins to snore.

"What's in that stuff?" asks Tonya.

Neither Boyo nor Sam answer – they are too busy trying to figure out how to squeeze past the guard without waking him up. As it turns out, they don't need to worry. The guard doesn't even flinch when Sam accidentally steps on his sleep-heavy arm.

"He'll probably have a bruise in the morning," says Sam. "But at least he won't remember where he got it."

Tonya runs ahead of the others. She scurries down the corridor like a rat in a familiar cage. Sam and Boyo exchange glances. *Doesn't Tonya seem a bit too much at home?*

"Hurry up," Tonya hisses from the doorway ahead of them. "Do you want them to catch you?"

Sam shivers. A picture of the giant called Lug springs to her mind. She is certain she will die if he so much as breathes on her. Suddenly, the full weight of the situation hits her. What are they doing here, anyway? What if they get caught? But there's no time to think about that. She hurries to catch up.

Tonya opens the door. Sam and Boyo follow her onto a catwalk that overlooks the factory floor. From their high perch, they can see the equipment down below: about a dozen shiny, steel machines. As they watch, Lug himself enters the factory, followed by three of his men.

Instantly, the foul smell of the men waft up to the catwalk.

"Get ready," Tonya whispers, plugging her ears with her fingers. The other two follow suit, and not a moment too soon. The machines kick into motion with the thunder of a freight train clattering over cold steel tracks. The noise shakes the brains in their heads, chatters their teeth and rattles their bones.

One of the machines begins to spit out plastic bottles. A mechanical arm holds up a bottle as another machine swivels over and fills it with water. Each full bottle rolls down the conveyor belt and drops neatly into place in a cardboard box. As each box fills with bottles, it is replaced with another box, and another, and another, and another.

"They must be draining the whole stream!" whispers Sam.

"And the lake," says Boyo. "All of our precious water."

Tears well up in Sam's eyes. She thinks about the stream that used to flow through her backyard. It's simply too horrible to think that it would now be strangled to death, after all the work the scientists had done to save it.

Tonya yawns, indifferent to the production line and what it might mean to the colony. "Let's go," she says. "While the machines are on, they'll never hear us." She leads the way to a room just off the catwalk.

Inside the room, Sam sees banks of light and power switches, all pushed to "on." She blinks. The room is so bright that everything seems brilliant yellow – from the walls to the floors to their own faces. The light radiates from a clear glass box that holds a crescent-shaped glowing flame.

"The power source," says Tonya.

"The missing slice of the sun!" Sam stares at the flame, mesmerized.

The thermostat on the wall shows 104 degrees Fahrenheit. Sweat drips from their faces. "So, before we burn up," says Tonya, "does anyone have any ideas how we can get this out of here?"

Now, this is a real dilemma. Sam inches a bit closer to the glass box but stops when she feels her eyebrows starting to sizzle. Suddenly she brightens. "What about the rainbow spray?"

"I already thought of that that, dummy," says Tonya. "But it's only good for two seconds, long enough to pass through the flames. We need to hold onto this for much longer."

"We'll find a way," says Boyo. "But we'll have to do our thinking somewhere cooler."

Sam would have liked to investigate some of the other switches and gadgets, but she is afraid she would melt into a puddle. "We're out of here," she says. "But we'll be back."

———

Now that they are out of the factory, back in the fresh air, they are all lighthearted. And proud of themselves — after all, they've discovered the missing piece of the sun, out-smarted the giants, and lived to tell the story.

"I can't wait to tell the Great Hildinski," Sam says, skipping down the path toward the magnetic train station.

Tonya stops in her tracks. "Are you nuts?"

"What?"

"You tell the Great Hildinski over my dead body."

"That could be arranged," interrupts Boyo, but of course, Tonya can't hear him. And Sam wisely chooses to ignore the remark.

"But we found the missing slice of sun! She's going to be so proud of us. Maybe there will be a reward."

"Don't kid yourself," Tonya scoffs. "That old trickster will take you for everything you're worth. She's not the one we're going to tell."

"Who else is there?"

"Why, Lug, of course."

"Are you nuts? He's the one we're going to steal the sun back from."

"Exactly." Tonya grins.

What? This makes no sense whatsoever.

"Do I have to spell it out for you?" Tonya continues. "Lug needs the sun to run the factory. He'll do anything to get it back."

"Yeah, like kill us."

"Not if we're smart. And I know I'm smart, although I'm not so sure about you two."

"Dead smart, that's what you'll be. Or should I say just dead?"

"Dead, schmead," mimics Tonya. "You're always so melodramatic."

"This is crazy," says Boyo. "The sun doesn't belong to us. It belongs to the colony."

Of course, Tonya can't hear Boyo and she wouldn't listen if she could. "The reason this will work is that our price is right," she says. "We're not going to get greedy. All we are asking is safe escort to up above."

"You don't have to do this, Sam," says Boyo. "Don't listen to her. The Great Hildinski will help you get home."

"She hasn't helped me very much so far," says Sam. But even as she says this, she wonders if this is true. After all, the old woman did tell her that there were three lessons and she has barely mastered the first one. Is she giving up too soon?

"You're right," says Tonya. "The Fake Hildinski hasn't helped you one bit. And she won't."

Who to believe? Would the Great Hildinski ever really help her find her way home? Or was Tonya's crazy plan her only chance?

Sam sighs. Suddenly, she doesn't feel well. Could she actually cheat and steal to get back home? Could she sell the sun, knowing that it is essential to the colony's survival? She shuts her eyes. On the back of her eyelids, she sees her Mom and Dad, clear as day. They both shake their heads, sadly.

She knows one thing for sure. She can't stand that look of disappointment on their faces, even if her dead parents are just a figment of her imagination.

Suddenly, she knows what she has to do. It's time to learn about lessons two and three. And then decide the best thing to do.

CHAPTER 13

Facing the Great Hildinski

What the kids don't know is that someone above ground is thinking about water too.

General Hoodwink stands in front of his map of the world, sticking in pins. "There," he says, jabbing a pin into a country neighboring his own. "They're short of water. They'll be begging for mercy soon."

He picks up the contract lying on his desk and looks at it. The letterhead says "Under-Under Water Factory." He nods happily.

"A deal at twice the price. With this stuff, I can take over the world."

He grabs a bottle, rips off the lid, and raises it in a toast. "To me!" he says, admiring himself in the mirror. "To my genius!"

Outside his castle, throughout the whole country, no one else has access to water like this. Some of his people boil the brown stuff that drips out of the faucet, ridding it of harmful bacteria. Others scrounge for half-empty plastic bottles left in alleys. Still others carry buckets for a long, long distance to get what they need.

But that's not something General Hoodwink particularly cares about. Not at all. He has purchased earplugs to shut out the sound of human misery.

————

Back in Under-Under, Sam opens the door to Simon and Grace's house to find Darby blocking the entrance way. He slams the door in her face.

Fantastic. As if she didn't have enough problems on her hands. She pushes her way in through the door.

"Who spit on your cornflakes?" she asks.

"You're nasty," Darby answers. "Nasty, nasty, nasty."

"Oh, I see," says Sam. "When I wash your dirty clothes, is that when I'm nasty? Or when I make your sandwiches? Tell me, and I'll be happy to quit."

"You left me behind."

All of a sudden, Sam feels terrible. It's true — she did leave him behind. Not on purpose, of course, but he still would feel abandoned, alone, and lonely. And she knows exactly what that's like.

"And you didn't even ask me about my adventure. Not once since I got here. Everything is always about you."

Adventure? What adventure?

"See?" says Darby. "You don't even know what I'm talking about. Well, for your information, I managed to find my way down to Under-Under by myself. Without your help."

This is true. He had managed to make his way down here somehow. And she hadn't even thought to ask how. All she had thought about when he arrived was the fact that he'd forgotten his medicine.

It must have been scary for him in the Underworld, just like it had been scary for her. He had gone through all of that too — on his very own journey.

"So tell me now," she asks gently.

"No." Darby juts out his lower lip, turns on his heel, and marches out of the room.

Grace walks in, with a question on her face.

"None of your business!" Sam yells before Grace can ask.

"All right," says Grace, brushing her soft fingers across Sam's cheek. "As long as you're both okay, that's all that's important."

How could Grace always be so good and kind? Sam wants to throw herself into those motherly arms and soak up some comfort. She can imagine feeling Grace's steady heartbeat next to her chest and breathing in her soft, sweet scent.

Perhaps Grace senses what Sam is thinking, because she reaches out and gives her a big hug. Instantly, Sam stiffens. It's way too scary to let someone get that close. No way.

Still, she is sad when Grace softly lets her go.

———

Darby strikes an awfully hard bargain.

"No, you can't come with us back to the factory," Sam says, stomping her foot. "Absolutely not." Sam has told him how they took the magnetic train, fed sleepy food to the guard, watched the noisy water-bottling machines, and discovered the missing slice of the sun. She told him all of this to make him feel included, but it had just the opposite effect.

"You have all the fun," he complains. "It's not fair."

"But Darby, it's dangerous."

"Then I should be there to protect you."

Sam smiles. He's a sweet kid but still just a kid. No way should she put him in danger. And no way did she think that he was really capable of doing anything to help.

"You think I can't take care of myself," continues Darby, as if reading her mind. "But you forget. Gemini and I made it down here all by ourselves. And we managed it without getting all wet the way that you did."

Now, Sam is curious. She remembers her own terrifying ride down the waterfall and into the lake. It's true that when Darby and Gemini arrived, neither one had been wet. "Okay, I'll bite. How did you manage that?" she asked.

Darby smiles smugly. "Strategy," he says, tapping his index finger against his head. "Instead of falling into the waterfall, I held onto Gemini. She jumped clear of the water and landed on a path right behind."

Trust Darby to find the easy way. Some people are just born lucky. Why is it she always has to do the hard stuff? And *Darby* says he doesn't think life is fair!

"So I'm coming along," he insists, "whether you like it or not."

Sam opens her mouth to argue but doesn't get a chance. Simon taps her on the shoulder. "I've come to get you, Sam. You're wanted at the palace."

A shiver runs up Sam's spine. Has someone told the Great Hildinski that they discovered the missing piece of sun... and failed to report it? Or has the old woman learned that she and Tonya broke into her private rooms in the palace?

Sam trudges toward the palace like a prisoner facing execution. Simon is about as kind a man as you could ever meet, but he keeps a firm grip on her elbow, steering her toward the palace more quickly than her legs want to carry her.

"Do you know why she wants to see me?"

"No," answers Simon. "But I doubt that she's asking you to tea."

The icy pit in her stomach grows even colder.

When they reach the palace, Simon pushes a button. Instantly, a section of the ring of fire is extinguished. This may be a less dramatic way to enter, but Sam has to admit that it is a whole lot less stressful.

Before she knows it, she faces the Great Hildinski herself.

The old woman's eyes blaze with fury. She stomps her wooden leg, shaking the room and everything in it. Paintings fly from the walls and crash to the floor. The raven swoops around the room, cawing madly. Sam's teeth rattle in her head.

This is not going to be easy. A knot forms in her stomach.

———

"You don't deserve my compassion. You're a liar and a sneak."

Sam swallows hard. This is her moment of decision. Tonya will be furious if she tells the Great Hildinski about their discovery. She'll call her a traitor and stop helping her find a way home. But on the other hand, if she holds back the truth, she won't be able to live with herself.

"I didn't steal the sun. But I know where it is."

She tells the whole story to the Great Hildinski. Then for a long moment, they are both silent. Finally, the old woman speaks.

"Tonya," she says. "She'd been in the factory before?"

Sam hesitates. This is the part she's been dreading. She doesn't want to rat on Tonya, but she wants to tell the truth. Sam squirms uncomfortably, trying to find a way to answer.

"Ah, I see."

It's hard to hide anything from the Great Hildinski.

"I know Tonya. I raised her after her parents ran away to up above."

Tonya hadn't told her anything about this. "So you're her grandmother?"

"No. I was married to her grandfather, but he had been married before. Tonya's mother was a troubled girl — and the apple doesn't fall far from the tree."

Sam wonders what Tonya will do to her when she learns that she has spilled the beans. She sighs deeply.

"By the way," says the Great Hildinski, cutting into her thoughts. "Did you find what you were looking for in my private apartment?"

Sam's mouth drops open. The Great Hildinski has known all along! Her face burns with shame. Now, how can she expect the old woman to help her go home?

"Come," says the Great Hildinski, standing up.

"To the dungeon?" She's not sure she wants to know the answer. Already, she can't breathe just thinking about the rats and spiders and other slimy things living there in the dark.

"To the forest."

"You're going to throw me to the wolves?"

The Great Hildinski cocks her head, apparently considering this suggestion very deeply. "Not today," she says.

Sam stands up reluctantly. If not wolves, then what?

In an instant, the Great Hildinski disappears through the doorway and Sam scurries to follow.

———

Sam creeps across the room. Not a squeak, not a crackle, not a sound. This is the first time she has managed this - and it feels wonderful.

"You are precisely there," announces the Great Hildinski, pointing an ancient finger directly at Sam and bursting Sam's bubble.

"Don't be discouraged," the old woman says, opening her eyes. "That wasn't bad for a beginner. But remember, this is just a small part of it. You need to learn to fully use all of your senses."

"But how do I do that?" It's impossible.

"You can do it. Just trust your body. Your body knows more than you think."

"Yeah, right. Why don't we just go to lessons two and three? They're probably not so hard."

"You may find them even harder." The old woman cups Sam's face in her hands. "But they are lessons you need to learn, my child. They are lessons you need, not just to get home, but for the rest of your life."

"But how am I supposed to learn all of this so quickly? I can't stay down here forever."

"Sometimes," says the old wise one, "people learn very quickly when they are put in a sticky situation."

Later, Sam would think that the Great Hildinski must have seen the future — because things quickly became very sticky indeed.

CHAPTER 14

The Next Theft

If a person could look like a fire-spitting dragon, that person would be Tonya and the moment would be now.

"What do you *mean* you told the Great Hildinski?!" she screeches. "You scum. You foul-breathed, rat-eating, garbage-licking, scab-picking, putrid, poor excuse for something I'd wipe off my shoes—*scum!*"

Sam hangs her head.

"And those are your good points!"

"I had to do it," Sam explains. "She knew most of it already anyway."

"Blah, blah, blah," says Tonya. "You're gutless, that's what you are. One teensy little question from the Great Old Fake and poor little Sam begs for mercy."

"Think whatever you want." Sam has taken just about enough. "Whether you like it or not, this is how things stand."

Tonya paces around the room. Finally, she throws her shoulders back and faces Sam. "You're lucky you're dealing with royalty," she says. "Because I'm so generous, I'll give you a second chance."

Don't do me any favors.

"What we need now is a new plan," announces Tonya. "Our best bet is to steal back the sun, and then return it to my step-grandmother. She'll be so grateful, she's sure to give us a reward, even if she is a stingy old bat."

Sam is tempted to point out that she'd wanted to do this in the first place but she doesn't want to set off another round of Tonya fireworks, so she keeps her lip zipped.

"I have to warn you," continues Tonya, "she's not going to want me to go up above with you. But I'll find a way."

Sam isn't at all sure that she wants Tonya to go up above with her. Would Tonya expect to live with her and Darby and Aunt C?

"Oh, don't expect me to stick around once we get above the ground," laughs Tonya. "I have a feeling that your life would be a little... how should I say it? Slow." Tonya gets a dreamy look in her eyes. "I'm going to go to nightclubs. And race tracks. I'm going to have fast cars, and cool clothes, and rich friends, and money, lots and lots of money." She throws back her head and laughs a particularly shrill sort of laugh.

"We'll get started in the morning," she says, almost pushing Sam out the door.

But she's wrong. Because morning never comes.

———

At noon the next day, Under-Under is still plunged in darkness. And everyone is still in bed. Accustomed to getting up at the first light, the citizens just roll over and snooze some more. Those who do venture out of bed get a nasty surprise: when they flick on their light switches, nothing happens.

"Must get new light bulbs in the morning," they think, sliding back between the covers. Not until the red alert gong thunders through the colony do people realize that something is horribly, dangerously wrong.

People bump around their houses, groping blindly for candles, tripping over their furniture and trying to locate their clocks. When finally, they see the time, they are startled to learn that they have slept for a full fourteen hours.

And the sky is still as black as the tar on the streets of Hades.

Of course, it is the Great Hildinski who puts two and two together. She understands that the entire sun has now been stolen — and thanks to Sam, she knows who has stolen it. She throws the whole weight of her body against the emergency gong, crashing into it like a missile striking a target. KA-RONG! Teeth shake in peoples' heads. Even the fish in the lake wobble like jelly.

It takes a bit of time for the adults to light their candles, gather up all of their family members, find their socks and shoes, and trundle down to the town square outside the palace. Then they have to make speeches, debate whose job it is to do what, elect a committee, and vote on the plan.

While all this is going on, Sam, Boyo, Tonya and Darby grab each other by the elbows and race toward the far end of the colony. Leading them is Gemini, whose white fur reflects the light from their candles and glows bright.

———

Unsupervised in the dark, the kids roll around in all directions like loose marbles, laughing with glee. Then Boyo's flashlight lights up the clock tower -- and the giggling immediately stops.

The soft light from the clock's friendly face has been snuffed out. One hand points at twelve, but the other arm is broken at the joint and rocks back and forth like a dead man swinging from the gallows.

Seeing the broken clock suddenly makes Sam very afraid.

Now, the kids start to squabble. Boyo doesn't want Tonya along (because he doesn't trust her). Tonya doesn't want Boyo along (because she thinks he's stupid), Sam doesn't want Darby along (because she thinks it's too dangerous). And Gemini blames all of them for forgetting to bring her dinner.

Tonya stirs the pot even more by latching onto Darby like she owns him. And Darby likes it! Every time he makes a silly joke, Tonya laughs and laughs and laughs – which makes smoke come out of Sam's ears because Darby isn't really that funny. "Hahahahaha", Sam scoffs but Tonya pretends she can't hear.

Then Sam starts to get cranky with Boyo. He jabbers away at her in the language that only she can understand, which makes it almost impossible for her to eavesdrop on Tonya and Darby. "Stop that!" she barks.

"Why listen to Tonya anyway?" asks Boyo. "She never has anything worthwhile to say."

Sam doesn't want to admit that she's maybe just a wee bit jealous. "Well," she shoots back," at least she's cool. Not like you and your stupid fish."

The look of hurt on Boyo's face cuts her to the quick. She can't stand it, so she storms away from the camp. But on her own, she feels even worse. She knows it's her own fault that she's all alone. And the longer she walks by herself, the smaller she feels, until she is just a speck on the landscape that could blow away with the slightest puff of wind.

That's when she remembers the Great Hildinski's lessons. "Trust your body," the old woman had said the first time they had talked about the way home. That part was hard enough but it was child's play compared to the next lessons.

She had been about to leave the palace yesterday when the Great Hildinski put her withered hand around Sam's arms and felt the tension between her shoulder blades. "You'll never be strong enough to make it home unless you do something about this," she had said.

Sam felt her body tensing even more. Of course, her shoulders were tight. She had a lot to worry about, in case the old lady didn't know it: stuck far from home, worried about her brother getting sick, afraid that Aunt C had done something stupid with The People, nervous that Tonya would get back at her for spilling the beans to the Great Hildinski, terrified that the ugly, smelly Lug would catch her in his huge, meaty hands. Of course, she was tense!

"You don't understand," Sam wailed. "Everything is easy for you. You have all the wisdom of your people and all the brains of the scientists on your side." Sam punched her hand against the stone wall. Her knuckles smarted, but somehow it felt good.

"Don't hurt yourself, child. That's not the way to do it."

Sam glared at the old woman, not sure whether to listen or to bolt. The Great Hildinski's eyes were as soft as feathers, as warm as a woolen blanket, but still they scared Sam.

"I hope you're ready," continued the Great Hildinski. "Because I can see that you need to know the last two lessons."

Sam waited. Here, at last, was her ticket home. She would pay close attention, memorize these tricks, grab her brother, and say goodbye. But as it turned out, it wasn't quite like that.

———

Walking alone along the dark path, Sam remembers how she had felt when she left the palace after learning about the lessons. "Empty" was one word that came to mind. "Discouraged" was another. Because the lessons weren't tricks after all — not like standing on one foot, or saying a magic formula, or pulling a rabbit out of a hat.

"The second lesson," said the Great Hildinski, "is to trust others."

"Great," thought Sam. "I've come all the way for this."

"I know what you're thinking," continued the Great Hildinski. "But it's harder than it sounds. Particularly since you have to learn who to trust."

"That part is easy," thought Sam. She doesn't trust anyone.

The ancient woman seemed to read her mind. "If you don't trust others, you will never find your way home."

"And what about the final lesson?" challenged Sam.

"The final lesson," answered the Great Hildinski, "is to trust yourself." *Trust others. Trust yourself.* What kind of lessons were these? Sam left the palace wishing she had never listened to the Great Hildinski in the first place.

But now, creeping through the silent trees with the blackness licking her face, Sam thinks again about the lessons. She needs something to hang onto. *But where to start?* How to trust? And who?

It's so dark, she can't even see the others ahead. Perhaps she's fallen so far back that she'll never find them. Perhaps she has already missed her chance to learn the second lesson.

Sam runs to catch up.

CHAPTER 15

Ready for Battle

Being in darkness all day and night scrambles your senses. You think something lies in one direction, when it is in exactly the opposite place. You think that any minute, the blackness will thin to reveal a brilliant orange sunrise, but it never does. *You think you know your way, but all the bread crumbs leading you there are gone.*

Feeling her way through the darkness, she has to be more open than she has ever been in her life. She rubs her forehead, trying to relax her brain. Then she lets her senses take over: smelling the slight acid scent of the factory, hearing just the faintest whir of machinery in the distance, feeling the echo of the bottling rhythm in the dirt beneath her feet. "It's that way!" she exclaims, pointing her finger straight into the blackness.

"You're crazy," says Tonya. "I say we go this way." She points as far away from Sam's spot as possible.

"Don't listen to her," warns Boyo. "You've got it right."

Sam holds her candle close to Boyo's face so that she can look into his eyes. She sees forgiveness there — something she isn't sure she deserves. "I'm sorry," she says out loud, even though she has the feeling he knows this already.

"Good," said Tonya, thinking that Sam has spoken to her. "I'm glad you're finally sorry about something. We'll go my way."

"No," insists Sam. "We won't."

In the end, it is Gemini who settles the matter. She leaps away, heading exactly in the direction that Sam has chosen. Fortunately, Tonya is so confused by this time that she thinks the cat has taken her side — so everybody is happy.

When they light a campfire, things suddenly get quite jolly. They forget who didn't want whom - to come. They all huddle together near the crackling fire and dream about the future. As long as they are warm and cozy, they assume that victory will be theirs.

"I'm going to drive a car so fast my hair flies straight backwards!" Tonya says with shiny eyes. "The smell of tar. Burning rubber. Gasoline. It's going to be heaven."

"But what if you crash?" Darby asks.

"Even better!" exclaims Tonya. "That's not something you can do on the magnetic train, with all their silly safety standards."

"I'm going to get a new bike with a gazillion speeds," declares Darby. "If I'm big enough to survive in another world, I'm big enough to get around by myself at home!"

Sam wisely decides not to challenge Darby on this. She knows they don't have the money for a new bike — not with Aunt C too sick to hold down a job. But there's no point spoiling the mood over details.

"I'm going to find a new doctor for Aunt C," Sam says. Maybe if they can find a cure for Aunt C, they could eventually get enough money for a bike? She figures while they're dreaming, she may as well dream big.

"So, why do you live with your silly old aunt anyways?" asks Tonya. "Don't you have parents?"

"No," replies Sam, suddenly solemn. "We don't."

"We used to live with a family called the McFlnts," Darby volunteers. "They were so mean and cheap, they wouldn't even spend a dime on a vowel for their own last name."

"They locked us in the cellar and made us carve toothpicks," adds Sam.

"Then we went to the O'Snagglety's. They took us in so they could snag more stuff. With the money they got for keeping us, they snagged a new television and a refrigerator..."

"And a boat!"

"Yes, a boat!" Darby chimes in. "Even though they live in the desert. Mr. O'Snagglety figured if he snagged a boat, he could snag an ocean."

Sam can see that Tonya is impressed. She and Darby have lived through plenty of stuff that would make other kids fall apart. "And then we got thrown in with the stray dogs," Sam concludes.

Boyo squeezes Sam's hand. Automatically, she starts to pull away but he grips her hand even tighter. She forces herself to relax. *Trust others.* His hand feels warm and comforting in hers. She is letting a boy – a cute boy – hold her hand!

But she can't let Tonya see. She gives Boyo's hand a quick squeeze and then gently pulls away. "One of the dogs bit me," she says, showing a scar on her arm.

Sam remembers how Aunt C had come to rescue them. She had marched into the dog pound, sporting her best hat and pearl necklace, quivering with indignation. "Those two would be mine," she had said firmly, pointing at Darby and Sam. After that, they had gone to live with Aunt C — which had been wonderful until the old dear had started to forget.

Sam shakes her head, clearing away the cobwebs of the past. No point dwelling on things that are already finished. She needs to have all of her wits about her now.

She has a job to do.

———

It's a good thing Sam doesn't know what's happening back at home — because if she did, she would feel even more anxious. General Hoodwink invaded the country next door, promising them water if they met his demands and then going back on that promise.

Now, everyone is tired, thirsty, sick, and desperate.

Aunt C sits by her radio, waiting for any little bit of good news. It doesn't come. She wants to join the protests against General Hoodwink, even though she knows she will go to jail for it. She wouldn't care about that so much — but she does care about what would happen to Sam and Darby.

And she can't leave the house anyway until she knows where the kids are.

She picks up the newspaper but quickly throws it away in disgust. The whole thing is full of praise for General Hoodwink's Under the Rug Plan. What a load of rubbish!

She looks outside at the grey sooty sky and wonders how anyone could possibly believe that this country is 'green.'

———

Sam tries to figure out if the other kids are ready. Now that it's time to attack the factory, they aren't quite so eager. "Why don't we wait till morning?" Tonya suggests, pulling herself a little closer to the fire.

"There's only one problem with that plan," Sam answers. "Without the sun, morning never comes."

"Maybe it will tomorrow?" Darby offers hopefully. After begging to be included in this adventure, it seems that he is now getting cold feet.

"Here's what we'll do," says Sam, tapping her walking stick into the ground just like she'd seen the Great Hildinski tap her wooden leg. Doing this gives her an air of authority. "We'll make a list of all of our special gifts and talents. Then we'll make a plan. So, who's first?"

"I can solve puzzles," volunteers Darby. After all the time he'd spent in bed, sick with fever, he'd learned to figure out how things worked.

"Good. And Boyo can hear even the tiniest sound," says Sam. "Plus, he's so quiet, he can sneak in anywhere."

"And Gemini has sharp claws," Darby adds. "Those have to come in useful."

"I can distract attention," offers Tonya. "It will be easy. After all, they know me."

All eyes turn toward Tonya. It is suddenly quiet enough to hear a bird rustle in the trees. "What do you mean, they know you?" Sam asks finally.

"I've been watching the factory for a while, you know," Tonya says defensively. "While you guys were just goofing off."

"So, Lug is a friend of yours?" This question is so important that Sam is afraid to breathe.

"Of course not," answers Tonya irritably. "But they know that I like to hang around the Far End. I think they kinda like me. So put me down as the person who will get their attention."

"Why didn't she tell us that the first time?" asks Boyo. "It would have made it a lot easier than giving the guard sleepy food."

Sam ignores Boyo. This is not the time to look backward, but to go forward. "And I am good at remembering," she concludes. "So we have puzzle solving, hearing, quietness, sharp claws, attracting attention, and remembering."

Not a bad list, thinks Sam — unless you're going up against big, smelly giants who might even have weapons. A cold lump settles into the pit of her stomach.

No one else looks like they're planning to lead this charge. It is going to be up to her.

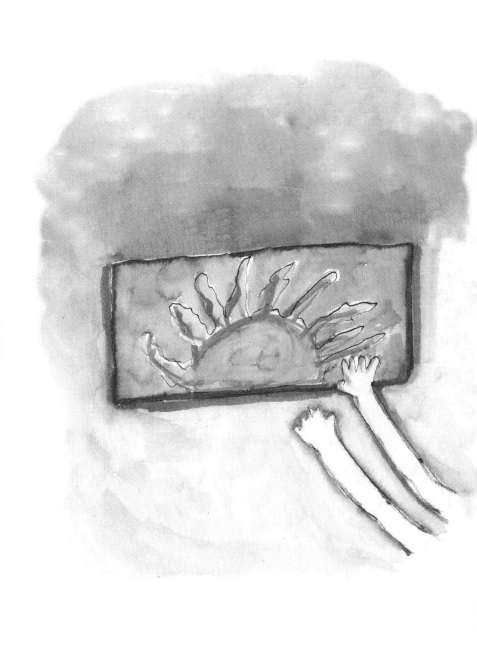

CHAPTER 16

Inside the Factory

Before Sam can fight the battle with the giants, she has to fight the battle within herself. "You can't do it!" a little voice shrieks. "Turn back while there's still time!"

She has some serious doubts. How would they get past Lug and his men? He could squish them between two of his fingers, stomp on them with his enormous boots, fry them with a jolt from the equipment, or just plain torture them to death with his rancid breath. And even if they did somehow manage to get past him, how on earth would they recapture the sun when it's far too hot to touch?

"But if you don't continue," argues another voice in her head, "you'll never find your way home."

First things first, thinks Sam. "Darby," she says. "You need to be ready for what's going to happen in the equipment room."

She hopes that Tonya can get them into the factory and that Boyo can stand guard. But the really tricky part will be in the equipment room where the sun is kept. She knows that they will only have a few minutes there, so they need to be ready to spring into action the second they make it through the door.

"Here's what I remember," Sam says to Darby. "The sun is in the middle of the room, but the key to opening it has to be in the side panels." She describes the three panels: each has seven rows of ten switches. The panel on the left has the switches all pushed to the right — so it must be the one that controls the power to the equipment. The middle panel has switches half on, half off. Sam assumes that this panel controls the lights in the building, as only some of the lights had been on when they were in the factory.

So if these assumptions are correct – and they had better be! – then the panel on the right must control the mechanism for unlocking the sun.

"It's in some kind of code," she explains to her brother. "So that's where you come in. Try to think about how you could use seventy switches to open the box."

There's another problem Sam must solve in advance: what to do once the box is open? "Boyo," she says. "I need your help."

As soon as the words are out of her mouth, she thinks of the Great Hildinski's second lesson: Trust others. It seems that this crisis is already helping her develop her skills. However, she doesn't have time to think about this right now.

Together, Sam and Boyo hunt until they find rosemary, peppermint, and other herbs that have a cooling effect. It's not easy searching by candlelight, and Sam has to try hard to be patient. "The slower you go, the faster you get there," she remembers Grace saying. If there's ever been a time to be calm, surely this was it.

Finally, they've collected enough herbs. Next, they peel long strips of dry bark off the black pine trees. They find the last little bit of river water – just a feeble trickle that escaped the big water pipes – and soak the bark in the water. When the bark is wet and spongy, they slather it with cooling herbs.

"Do you think it will hold?" asks Sam, anxiously.

"It had better," replies Boyo, trying hard not to look scared.

"All right, then," says Sam, standing up straight and tapping her stick on the ground. "Let's go."

———

You would think that things were just about as tough as they could get: four kids and a cat taking on four evil men who were at least ten times as big. But things suddenly get tougher. It starts to rain – not just little droplets, but a pelting, skin-soaking, rat-drowning downpour.

"I've never seen rain like this in Under-Under!" exclaims Sam.

"That's because it's usually on a timer," explains Boyo. "The scientists have it perfectly scheduled, but now with the sun gone, it looks like it's quit working."

The dirt on the pathway sloshes into mud. The mud splatters over their clothes, into their eyes, through their hair. It gets so deep in places, their boots get stuck in the gooey mess and sucked right off their feet. "Yikes!" yelps Darby, as his stockinged feet land smack in the muck.

Ahead, they see two of the giants heaving boxes from the factory onto a huge trolley outside. "Wish me luck," Tonya says, slipping away from the others and approaching the men.

Sam would have liked to stay and listen to what she said to them, but she knows that this is their only window of opportunity. "Now," she whispers to Boyo and Gemini. While Tonya positions her body to hide the back entrance, they slip through the door.

None of them are prepared for what they see inside. Light. Brilliant, dazzling light. Brighter than anything they have ever seen before, and particularly shocking after all the darkness outside. They stand blinking in the entryway, trying to adjust their eyes to the glaring light.

Now, it's Boyo's turn to take the lead. He makes them all stay very, very still – then listens. "One of them is on the factory floor," he tells Sam. "I can hear the other one breathing in the equipment room upstairs."

Sam nods, giving him the signal. Without making any sound whatsoever, Boyo creeps through the hallway to the factory floor. Right under the giant's nose, he switches the bottling machine to "off".

As the machine clanks and groans to a stop, Boyo sneaks back to join the others.

"Drat!" the giant bellows. "The stupid machine is broken!"

From upstairs, they hear a similar roar. The other giant must be discovering the flipped switch on the control panel. As Sam had predicted, he storms out of the equipment room and thunders down the stairs to investigate.

It's now or never.

Steering Darby by the elbow, Sam tiptoes up the stairs. Thankfully, the door was left swinging open. "Here," she says, pointing Darby toward the right-hand panel. "Work your magic."

Darby glides his fingers over the switches. Cautiously, he flicks one forward and sees that the back side is yellow. He pushes another one — this one is black. He chews the corner of his lip. He pushes one more switch — another black one.

"What does it mean?" Sam fidgets anxiously. She knows that standing over him won't help, but she also knows that they have very little time. She does not want to be in this room when the giant returns.

———

Darby's fingers are slippery as they fiddle with the switches. This puzzle is hard enough to solve without trying to do it in tropical heat. A big droplet of sweat plops from the end of his nose right onto the control panel, splashing the switches and making them even slipperier.

Sam bites her nails. She wants to shove her brother out of the way and do this task herself, except she knows Darby is the right person for this job. "Lesson number two, lesson number two," she chants in her head, trying to trust Darby even though it has already taken him ten painful minutes. And he doesn't seem any closer to a solution.

To make the waiting more bearable, she paces around the room. That's when she notices a valve, tucked way back in the corner. It has a skull and crossbones painted on it and a red warning, "Do not touch!" She inches closer, flaring her nostrils. There is a slight smell rising from it — a smell she recognizes from somewhere.

She sniffs again. Then the penny drops. Gas. Exactly the smell that she had noticed from time to time in their own backyard. She sees that the arm of the valve is pointing toward "on." Then she notices something even more scary. Under the "Do not touch!" sign is another message in smaller lettering: "Gas to Up Above." Below that, in even smaller lettering: "Gas to Sockeye Street. Highly toxic. Do not shut off."

Sam's head spins. Could the giants be poisoning them on purpose? Whatever the case, Sam isn't taking any chances. With a mighty heave, she shoves the arm of the valve to "off." Right away, she can hear the hissing of the gas sputter and die.

Now that she has discovered the valve, she wants to investigate more. But just then, she hears Darby catch his breath. She dashes to his side and looks down at the control panel. Where it had been just a mishmash of switches, there is now a picture: a brilliant yellow sun with rays pointing outward from the centre. All around it is black.

"You did it!" Sam exclaims. She watches as Darby flicks one last switch and then CLICK! The latch on the glass box springs open.

Now, it's her turn to work. She is just a wee bit nervous about this part. *No, take that back* – she is petrified. All very good to have the herb-cooled carrying basket ready, but first she needs to lift the scorching sun out of the box. She takes a deep breath.

Trust your body, trust your body. She imagines ice. Frosty blue ice and swirling snowflakes forming a white cloud. She feels her core getting colder, then takes another deep breath. The frost enters her lungs – and she exhales, pushing the cold towards her fingertips.

With icy blue hands, Sam reached into the box. Even though she sees that her fingers are frozen, even though she has decided to trust her body, she is terrified of getting burned. Can she really hold the sun with her bare hands? She musters all of her courage – grabs the sun in one swift motion and flings it into the carry basket before it can melt the frost off her hands.

She can't believe it. They have captured the sun!

Darby grins. "I knew you could do it!" he says in a proud voice that makes Sam remember why she loves him so much. But then the grin is suddenly wiped clean off his face.

Sam spins around. Lug towers in the doorway, baring his teeth as if he were a dog. She should have smelled him coming. In the moment of her victory, she had gotten sloppy. She had forgotten to stay alert with her senses, and now she would pay for it.

CHAPTER 17

In the Flames

There is no avoiding the stench of the giant now. Sam can actually see it in the air, great floating globules of grey greasy filth. She wants to shut her eyes so that the odor won't sting her eyeballs, but she doesn't dare. Lug lurches forward, wafting the evil smell closer and closer to the spot where she and Darby huddle.

The electric lights dim — then cut out. There must have been just enough juice in the system to keep them on for a minute after the sun was disconnected, but that power has now been sucked dry. The only light in the room comes from the sun itself, but it is a faint light, swaddled in the cool bark that seems to put its brilliance on snooze. From down below they hear crashing and clanging and shouting. The other giants must have been caught off guard when the blanket of darkness wrapped itself around them, making them stumble in their clumsy rubber boots.

Lug darts out a beefy hand and clutches Darby by the throat. Sam gasps as Lug lifts her brother up by the scruff of his neck, shaking him back and forth as if he were a rag doll. He could break Darby's neck this way! Desperate, Sam launches herself at the giant, kicking him in the ankles as hard as she could. But nothing seems to stop him. Now, Lug is laughing, a gurgling, nasty sort of laugh — as if killing a boy was the funniest thing he'd done in his whole life.

"Yeow!" the giant bellows, dropping Darby like a sack of unwanted potatoes. His huge ugly face contorts with pain.

It takes Sam a second to realize that Darby is free. It takes Darby even longer to realize this as he lies completely stunned on the floor. But when

Sam sees Gemini ripping into the giant's back, digging her claws in deeper and deeper, she gains a new sense of hope.

She drags Darby by the arm and bolts toward the door.

Her fingers touch the cold metal of the knob. She is almost there! But then an iron hand grips her ankle.

Over her shoulder, she sees Lug shimmying along the floor, with Gemini still attached to his back. He tightens his grip on her ankle.

Even Gemini isn't laughing now.

Sam stumbles, dropping the sun. She feels herself being dragged back, inch by inch. Desperate, she reaches her free hand for her walking stick — just beyond her grasp.

She sends all of her strength to her fingertips, stretching them out like new shoots on a tree. Another half an inch. Finally, she clutches the smooth wood of the stick in her hand and smacks Lug with all of her might.

She runs.

———

Somehow, all the kids find each other in the forest. They are still close enough to the factory to hear cursing and screaming as the giant men crash around the building in the dark.

Sam is relieved to see that Darby has the carry bag containing the sun. He must have picked it up from the factory floor where she dropped it. He beams, bright as the sun itself, proud of the role he has played in the capture.

But where is Gemini? Should she go back to the factory to find her? Sam hesitates... then sees a streak of white. When Gemini wraps her white tail around the girl's skinny ankles, Sam wants to kiss her. (Not that the cat would ever allow it). Gemini might have lost a claw or two to the giant's back, but she is none the worse for wear. She licks a dainty paw, as if the most important thing in the world is getting the evil giant smell off as quickly as possible.

Ka-BOOM! A mighty explosion and a thousand thunderbolts rip through the black sky. Fiery sparks shoot skyward like an insane geyser. All around them, bits of burning metal blaze to the ground, torching the earth wherever they land. A piece of burning ash lands not an inch from Gemini, sizzling the fur right off her tail and sending the cat screeching up in the air.

In the blink of an eye, they are surrounded by flames.

There's no time to think. On instinct, Sam reaches into Tonya's bulging pocket. Her fingers wrap around something smooth and cool. She wrenches it out, discovering that it is exactly what she had hoped for: a can of rainbow mist.

She tosses the can to Boyo. Quick as a thief, she pulls a second can from Tonya's pocket before the other girl even realizes what is happening.

"Pull the tab," commands Sam, "and stay together."

"Not without you," says Boyo, who has both Darby and Gemini safely tucked under his arm.

"I'm right behind you. We'll meet at the palace. Go now."

Still, Boyo hesitates — until Sam thumps out a warning with her stick. Reluctantly, Boyo opens the can and disappears into the sparkling rainbow mist.

The blazing flames creep closer to the girls. "Ready?" she asks Tonya.

Tonya wraps an arm around Sam, grabbing the sun so that Sam has her other hand free. Sam pulls the tab and the girls feel the cool wetness on their faces. They smell each delicious color of the rainbow: from spicy apple to orange, lemon, lime, blueberry, lavender, and grape. They emerge from the other side of the flames cool and refreshed.

Sam wants to take a minute to simply enjoy being alive, but Tonya will have none of it. "We have to keep going," she insists. "They have rainbow mist, too."

Sam raises an eyebrow. "How did they get the mist?" she asks.

Tonya shrugs, looking away.

If the giants can get through the flames, then Tonya is right—this is no time to slow down.

Tonya grabs Sam's hand, pulling her to her feet. They scramble through the forest and into the open meadow. "I know a place we can hide," Tonya says. "Just a little bit farther. Hurry."

Both girls pump their legs up and down like engine pistons as they sprint toward the edge of the meadow, hair streaming behind them.

"Faster!" commands Tonya, with what seems like the last of her breath. The landscape spins past so quickly, Sam can't even see where she is going. They streak across the meadow, gaining speed — running faster and faster and faster ...

Tonya suddenly lets go of her arm.

Sam sails through the air and crashes to the ground in a heap, smashing her nose against the hard dirt. Her face throbs with dull pain and she feels a needle-like sting from her left leg. What on earth happened? Had Tonya tripped? Why had she let go?

Then she hears it: a heavy, iron gate clanging shut.

———

The next thing Sam hears is screeching, crow-like laughter. "You," howls Tonya. "You are the dumbest girl I ever met."

Sam sees that her worst fear is in fact true. She is in a cage. Tonya has tricked her.

"What, you thought we were friends?" Tonya struts in front of the cage. "Give me a break."

Sam has always realized that Tonya had sharp features — sharp elbows in particular. But before this moment, she's never noticed that everything about the girl is pointed: ears, nose, and especially teeth. She wonders why she had ever thought this girl was cool. There is nothing attractive about her now.

"Here's my special surprise," Tonya continues, pulling another can out of her other pocket. Sam can see that this is not another can of rainbow mist, but something different.

Grinning, Tonya pulls back the tab.

Most all of Sam's senses are already on red alert. But now, her sense of smell kicks into overdrive. A horrible stink invades the air. But not just any stink. It's the same gas smell she had sniffed in the factory, the same revolting mixture of acid and rotting garbage. It is precisely the same smell she had first detected in her own backyard. She remembers the tiny sign in the equipment room: Highly toxic.

"This isn't funny, Tonya," she chokes.

"No? I think it's hysterical." Tonya covers her nose with a handkerchief and places the can closer to Sam. "I'm sorry I can't stay and chat," she says, "but I've got to take the sun back to Lug."

Sam's skin crawls. In that moment, she knows that Tonya means to kill her.

"You didn't think I was going to give it back to the Great Fake, did you? Really, Sam." Tonya backs away from the cage, careful not to breathe any of the poisonous air. "It didn't have to end this way, you know. If you had just minded your own business, you wouldn't be in this spot."

Sam presses her nose into her jacket. She has to talk Tonya into letting her go, and that means exposing herself to the deadly air. "You still need me," she whispers.

Tonya laughs. "I *did* need you," she admits. "But that was when I was desperate for a way to go up above. If only Lug had agreed to take me then, but he was too afraid of the old lady. Now that I have the sun, he can't say no."

"So you gave them the rainbow mist,"

"Of course. I helped them steal the stupid sun in the first place." Tonya has now moved so far away that Sam can barely hear her. "They really should have been more grateful. I am royalty, after all."

"You'll never get away with this. The Great Hildinski will stop you."

"You think so?" Tonya laughs again. "I'll be long gone before she finds you. And you'll be dead."

The sun in Tonya's hand is now so far away it is only a pinpoint in the blackness. Then Sam can't see it at all. "Goodbye, Sam!" calls Tonya from a distance.

Then she is all alone.

———

As wise as she is, the Great Hildinski was wrong about Tonya. The girl is *not* harmless. But for once, Sam doesn't get angry or punch the walls of the cage. She realizes that she is as much to blame as anybody — after all, there had been plenty of reasons why she shouldn't have trusted Tonya. She had ignored all the warnings instead of trusting her own instincts.

Unfortunately, she isn't going to live long enough to put this lesson to use.

She hasn't felt this alone or desperate since the day she learned her parents had died. Her babysitter had told her the news: her parents' boat had sunk while they were out on a secret environmental mission. No one knew why. "You have to be brave, Sam," she had said. "You need to make them proud of you."

Sam had clenched her fists. How dare they leave her alone? Who was going to show her how to be brave? She didn't know how! She had kicked over her mother's favorite rose plant, spraying dirt all over the floor. Then she locked herself in the bathroom, huddling against the cold tile and howling a silent scream that couldn't work its way into tears.

"You left me," she accuses her mother now, pressing herself against the hard wall of the cage.

Out of the velvet blackness comes a voice, soft as the night air itself. "I will never leave you Sam. Remember what I said? When you're in a tight spot, breathe."

Sam puts her handkerchief over her nose and breathes.

"And remember what I told you?" whispers another voice that sounds just like the Great Hildinski. "You're ready for the third lesson now. Trust yourself."

Trust herself? How? She's just a girl, and the bars on the cage are made of steel. What can she do?

The answer comes first to her fingertips. They start wiggling, all by themselves. "Help!" they say in the language that Boyo, the fish, and the sea creatures can understand. Of course, she can speak this language! It's worth a try.

She doesn't really know how this language works. Does she have to be in the same room? Or can her words pass through solid walls, through water, over obstacles, and around corners? "Help! Stop the thief! She's got the sun!" With a few quick taps of her fingers, she tells them everything.

She waits. And hopes. All she can hear is the sound of night crickets in the forest and, of course, the hissing of the gas leaking from the can.

She begins to despair and grow dizzy.

CRASH! A deafening noise rips through the stillness. SPLASH! More crashing. More splashing. A hundred explosions follow one after another, like a row of powder keg dominoes falling one at a time. A hundred dinosaurs thrashing their mighty tails couldn't make more noise.

Then, through all the clatter slices one shrill, high-pitched scream: Tonya's voice.

And then one final, girl-sized splash.

————

When Boyo and Darby arrive, they seize the can of gas and seal it in an airtight container. By this time, Sam is feeling weak. Through blurred eyes, she watches as they remove the poison and begin to saw through the heavy metal bars.

"You'll make it," says Boyo. "You're strong."

Sam closes her eyes, conserving her resources. She is too exhausted to be excited, but she feels an overwhelming sense of peace. Even though she knows she is still alone in the cage, she feels a hand squeezing her own.

As they cut through the final steel rod that imprisons her, Sam realizes that they have won. The sun has been rescued. She is still alive. And she has learned all three lessons.

She is ready now to go home.

Afterward

Saying goodbye to the people in Under-Under — especially her good friend Boyo — is the hardest thing Sam has ever done.

But it's time to go.

Everyone gives Sam a minute alone with the boy. When their fingers finally stop waving — when they can't stretch out the goodbye any longer — they give each other a big warm hug.

Sam is silent then as she walks up the path with The Great Hildinski. Darby and Gemini skip on ahead, already forgetting about this adventure in their eagerness to go home. But Sam is troubled.

"Will everything be okay now?" she asks the wise old woman. She knows that the immediate danger is past. Lug and his men will face trial and Tonya will be severely punished. No more will the girl roam free — now, she will be under constant supervision.

But Sam worries about the future. Could someone steal the sun and water again? Will something get in the way of the scientists' important work?

"I can't tell you for certain, my child," answers The Great Hildinski. "There will always be people with evil in their hearts." She cups Sam's face in her hands. "But what we must remember is that most people are good. And we must be good ourselves."

Sam feels a little bit better when the old woman tells her about the news from up above. Apparently, there's been a big scandal. A mob of thirsty people broke into General Hoodwink's castle and discovered that he had been diverting all the water, keeping it all for himself. So they redistributed the water and declared National Water Awareness Day to celebrate.

General Hoodwink refused to comment.

Tenderly, the Great Hildinski slips a necklace over Sam's head. On the chain is a tiny silver fish. "To remember us by," the old woman says.

And then as if by magic, she is gone.

Sam stands, blinking back the tears. As if she would ever forget! "Goodbye, Great Hildinski! Goodbye, everyone!" She looks back at the beautiful colony and the people she has grown to love.

"Goodbye, fish," she says, waving her fingers. She owes them a special debt — after all, they were the ones to save her. They had responded to her call for help by swarming the bridge while Tonya was trying to cross.

Sam wishes she could have seen it: hundreds of fish leaping in the air and then slapping their tails hard against the water. The sea boiled with churned-up waves, so forceful that the bridge rocked from side to side, making it impossible for Tonya to keep her balance. When she fell, the sun flew out of her arms and landed in a tree, safe within its bark casing.

"Goodbye, Sam!" call the fish. "Come see us again."

Now, the way home doesn't seem so difficult. Relaxing her eyes, she can see the dirt path hidden behind the waterfall. "Come on," she says to Darby and Gemini, allowing her body to lead the way home.

Aunt C spots them the second they pop up from the hole in the ground. But this is a different Aunt C than they remember. This one is wearing a spotless apron and clean, shiny pearls. This one (it turns out) is a very good cook, now that she no longer has trouble remembering. Now, (thanks to their adventure in Under-Under), the evil gas that caused her forgetfulness (and Darby's illness) is gone from their lives forever.

Even The People admit that Aunt C is capable of taking care of Sam and Darby without their help.

Of course, there are disadvantages as well. Now that Aunt C isn't forgetful, she reminds Sam and Darby about a whole bunch of pesky things: homework, piano lessons, making beds, finishing their plates at dinner, and showing respect to their elders (to name just a few.) No more setting their own bedtimes. No more chocolate bars for breakfast.

"Oh well," thinks Sam. "You can't have everything."

When you're in a tight spot, *breathe*.

THE END.

Author's Note

Secrets of the Under-Under World: Water is a work of fiction. Some of the problems in the book are real – like pollution and water shortages. Some things are imaginary – like the under-under sun, rainbow mist and the magnetic train. But these imaginary solutions are examples of what *could* be. And who knows what young people – with their brains, fresh thinking, and talent – can come up with to make the real world a better place?

To learn more about the series of *Under-Under World* books please visit underunderworld.com.

About the Author

P.S. Whatever lives in Vancouver, Canada and writes under the supervision of her two cats. Under her real name, she has written 24 television episodes of Lost Tales of the Brothers Grimm as well as other works of fiction and non-fiction. She is also a professional corporate writer and marketer.

Why does she write under a pen name? "I was born with one last name and traded it for another when I married," she explains. "I've gathered many nicknames, which I can change into and out of like clothes. I finally realized that I could name myself – at least while writing – so I chose a name that expressed infinite possibilities. *Whatever.* I can make my way in the world, as the person I want to be, and do *whatever* makes my heart sing. And so can you."

Made in the USA
Columbia, SC
08 April 2021